HEINEMANN GUIDED READERS

INTERMEDIATE LEVEL

Series Editor: John Milne

The Heinemann Guided Readers provide a choice of enjoyable reading material for learners of English. The series is published at four levels. At *Intermediate Level,* the control of content and language has the following main features:

Information Control   Information which is vital to the understanding of the story is presented in an easily assimilated manner and is repeated when necessary. Difficult allusion and metaphor are avoided and cultural backgrounds are made explicit.

Structure Control   Most of the structures used in the Readers will be familiar to students who have completed an elementary course of English. Other grammatical features may occur, but their use is made clear through context and reinforcement. This ensures that the reading as well as being enjoyable provides a continual learning situation for the students. Sentences are limited in most cases to a maximum of three clauses and within sentences there is a balanced use of adverbial and adjectival phrases. Great care is taken with pronoun reference.

Vocabulary Control   There is a basic vocabulary of approximately 1,600 words. At the same time, students are given some opportunity to meet new words whose meanings are either clear from the context or are explained in the *Glossary.* Help is also given to the students in the form of illustrations which are closely related to the text.

Guided Readers at Intermediate Level

Note on Difficult Words

Some difficult words and phrases in this book are important for understanding the story. Some of these words are explained in the story, some are shown in the pictures, and others are marked with a number like this . . . .¹. Words with a number are explained in the glossary on page 89.

Shane

JACK SCHAEFER

Rewritten by JOHN MILNE

Illustrated by David Knight

HEINEMANN EDUCATIONAL BOOKS
LONDON

Heinemann Educational Books Ltd
22 Bedford Square, London WC1B 3HH
LONDON   EDINBURGH   MELBOURNE   AUCKLAND
HONG KONG   SINGAPORE   KUALA LUMPUR   NEW DELHI
NAIROBI   JOHANNESBURG   IBADAN
KINGSTON   EXETER (NH)   PORT OF SPAIN

ISBN 0 435 27001 X

This version first published 1973
Reprinted with corrections 1975
Reprinted 1976, 1977, 1980

Cover by Bill Heyes

Set, printed and bound in Great Britain by
Cox & Wyman Ltd, Reading

Contents

Introductory Note

The people in this story lived in the West of North America in the last century. The first Europeans in North America settled on the East Coast.

Slowly people moved to the West. They found the large, empty grass plains. These plains were very good for breeding cattle.[1] The first settlers made very large farms which were called ranches.

The American Indians who had lived on the plains were forced back. In the end the Indians were given parts of the country where they had to live. They were not allowed to live anywhere else. The places where the Indians lived were called reservations.

⬤ The ranches had one owner and many other men worked for him. This owner might own a hundred square miles of land or even more. The land round the ranch was called the range. The cattle could wander all over the range and feed on the grass. Sometimes the owner did not own all the range. But he could use the land for his cattle, because no one else was using it.

At the time of this story, small farmers were moving in and buying their own land. They wanted to grow crops as well as keep cattle and they started to build fences. These farmers were called homesteaders.

This story, Shane, is told by a young boy called Bob. Bob's father is one of the homesteaders who has bought his own farm and has fenced it in.

In the valley where Bob lives there is a big farmer called Fletcher. Fletcher has his ranch on one side of the river. But Fletcher has also used the land on the other side of the river as an open range. The farm that Bob's father has built is between the river and open range. If more and more settlers come and make farms and put fences round them, Fletcher's cattle will not be able to get to the river to drink water. Then he will not be able to use that land behind the settlers' farms as an open range.

There are a few other homesteaders as well as Bob's father, but Bob's father is their leader. If Bob's father stays, then the other settlers will stay also. And more and more settlers will come into the valley and Fletcher will lose his land. This is why Fletcher wants Bob's father to leave the valley.

⬤ See the map on page 9.

1. The Mysterious Stranger

The mysterious stranger appeared one summer afternoon in 1889. I was only ten years old at the time and I was enjoying my long summer holiday. Most of the time I did nothing and enjoyed myself sitting in the sun.

That summer afternoon I was sitting in the sunshine on the upper rail of our small corral when I saw the stranger coming on horseback towards our house.

In the clear air, I could see him plainly although he was still several miles away. There seemed at first nothing unusual about him. He seemed like just another stranger riding up the road towards our town. Then I saw two cowboys[2] going past him. They stopped and stared after him very carefully.

As he came nearer, I noticed his clothes. He wore dark-coloured trousers and tall leather boots. He also wore a broad leather belt. His shirt was dark brown and his coat, made of the same dark material as his trousers, was thrown over his saddle in front of him.

He had a handkerchief of black silk knotted round his throat and his hat was unusual. It was made of a soft black material which I had never seen before. His hat had a wide brim which came down in front of his face.

None of his clothes looked new. They were covered with dust and looked old. Although I was so young – only ten as I said – I felt immediately interested in this stranger. The clothes he wore showed that he was unusual. They were old but he still looked proud.

When he came nearer, I was able to see him more clearly. I forgot about the clothes. I began to see the kind of man he was. I understood then why the two cowboys had looked at him so carefully. He was not very tall and he did not look very big and broad like my father. But he did look strong and powerful.

He had no beard or moustache. His face was lean and hard and it was burned with the sun. His eyes seemed covered by the broad brim of his hat. But as he came nearer, I could see that they were alert and looking for any danger. I could see that he was noticing everything that he passed. And he rode easily on his horse like a man who had lived in the saddle.

Suddenly I felt cold. I am not sure why because it was a warm day. But I think it was a feeling caused by this stranger. He looked mysterious and dangerous.

He stopped about twenty feet away from me. He looked at our house with his sharp eyes. It was a small wooden farmhouse of one storey. On one side there was the corral with its strong rails. It was big enough to hold about thirty head of cattle.[3] Behind the corral was the pasture with a strong fence round it. On the other side was the barn for storing our winter food for the cattle. Behind the house there was mother's kitchen garden where she grew the vegetables she used in her cooking. My mother was a very good cook.

The house was clean and tidy. And it was nicely painted in white with green round the edges. This was unusual in the place where we lived, but my mother wanted it to be like that.

The stranger looked at everything carefully. I could see that he noticed everything about the house and the farm. He particularly noticed the flowers that my mother had planted

beside the steps up to the porch. Then he had a good look at the shiny new pump.

I felt cold again without knowing why. Then he spoke to me and his voice was soft and gentle.

'Could I use your pump to get some water for myself and my horse?' he asked politely.

I was trying to think of a reply when I realized that the stranger was not speaking to me. He was speaking to my father who was standing behind me near the gate of the corral.

'Use all the water you want, stranger,' replied my father.

Father and I watched him get off his horse easily and skilfully. He led the horse over to the trough which he filled with water. He pumped the water into the trough until it was almost full and waited until the horse started to drink. Then he started to wash himself.

When he had finished washing, he put his shirt on again. Then he combed his hair carefully and tied the handkerchief round his neck and put on his hat. After that he walked over to mother's flowers. He picked one of the flowers and stuck the flower into his hatband. I was surprised by this. None of the men I knew took any interest in their appearance.

I began to admire this unusual man. I did not feel cold any longer. I already liked his hat and his boots and wanted to wear them myself.

He got on the horse and started moving towards the gate. As he passed us, he stopped the horse and looked down. His eyes were alert but they seemed to be smiling. And when he looked at you, his eyes became still and not restless. You knew that his whole attention was concentrated on you when he looked at you.

'Thank you,' he said in his gentle voice and he turned his horse to move away from us towards the road.

'Don't be in such a hurry, stranger,' said my father.

The stranger stopped his horse and looked round at father with his hard, alert eyes. I stared in wonder as father and the

5

stranger looked carefully at one another. I was too young to understand fully what was happening. But I felt that each was trying to understand the other – to decide what kind of person he was.

Then my father started to speak again. He was smiling and I knew from the way he spoke that he had made up his mind.[4] He had decided that he liked this stranger.

'Don't be in such a hurry, stranger,' my father said again. 'Food will be on the table soon. You can eat here and stay for the night.'

The stranger nodded quietly. He also had made up his mind.

'That's very kind of you,' he said. He jumped off his horse and walked towards us leading the horse behind him. Father walked beside him when he came up to us and together they walked to the barn. I followed closely behind.

'My name's Joe Starret,' said my father, 'and this is my son, Bob.'

The stranger nodded again.

'Call me Shane,' he said. Then he turned to me. 'So your name's Bob,' he said. 'Well, Bob, I noticed you watched me very carefully as I came up the road. That's a good thing to do. A man who watches carefully what's going on around him will do well in life.'

Shane knew what to say to please a boy. I had started to admire him. But now he became my hero.

He let me help him look after his horse. Shane put his horse in the barn and I helped him. But I did notice something unusual. When I reached for his saddle-roll,[5] he stopped me He picked up the saddle-roll himself and put it on a shelf.

When the three of us arrived at the house, mother was waiting for us. And I noticed that she had already put an extra plate on the table.

'I saw you through the window,' she said to Shane.

'Marian' (that's my mother's name), my father said, 'I'd like you to meet Mr Shane.'

'Good evening, ma'am,' said our visitor.

'And good evening to you, Mr Shane,' replied mother. 'If Joe hadn't called you back, I would have done it myself. You won't find better food up the valley than you will here.'

As I said before, mother was an excellent cook. She really was and she knew it and was proud of it.

My mother was a strange woman in many ways. She had come from the East of America where things were more civilized and she was proud of that too. She liked to think that she kept a really good house for my father and me. And she did too. Father and I were very proud of her. In my eyes, she was the best woman in the world.

Then we moved into the house to have our supper.

POINTS FOR UNDERSTANDING

1. Who was Bob and where did he live?
2. Why did Bob suddenly feel cold?
3. Why did the stranger stop at the farm?
4. Why did Bob's father invite the stranger to stay?
5. What happened when Bob reached for the saddle roll?

2. Serious Conversation

We sat down to an excellent supper and I listened to the conversation. Both father and mother were trying to ask questions so that Shane would tell them something about himself. They were doing it very politely and hoping that Shane would not notice. But I also understood that Shane knew what they were trying to do. He answered all their questions very politely but he did not tell them anything about himself.

7

Shane must have been riding for many days, because he had lots of news about different towns. Some of the towns were so far away that I had never even heard of them before. He spoke a lot about the towns, but he said nothing about himself.

After we all had eaten, mother washed the dishes in the kitchen and I dried them. The two men went out, and sat on the porch. When I had finished my work in the kitchen, I went outside and sat on the edge of the porch and listened to them talking.

Our visitor was clever and made father do most of the talking. Father talked about his difficulties on the farm and about his plans for the future. Our visitor sat back and let him talk.

*'Yes, Shane,' I could hear my father say, 'A lot of farmers are buying land and building fences round their land. The fence lines are closing in. The open range can't last for ever. The trouble with open range is that you use a lot of space but you do not make very much money. Some people can't understand that yet. They will some day.'

Shane grunted, but I could not decide whether he agreed or not. Father went on talking.

'The only person who makes money from open range is the really big rancher. And even he doesn't make a lot of money nowadays. Things are going to change and a lot more small ranchers like myself will be putting up fences.'

'Well, now,' said Shane, 'that's very interesting. I've heard many clever men say the same as you are saying. Perhaps there's some truth in it.'

'There's plenty of truth in it,' replied my father strongly. 'Listen to me, Shane. The thing to do is to choose your piece of land and buy it. Then it is your own and you are not paying any money to a landlord.[6] Grow enough crops to give you

---

* This conversation is a very important one. Read the Introductory Note again on page v.

8

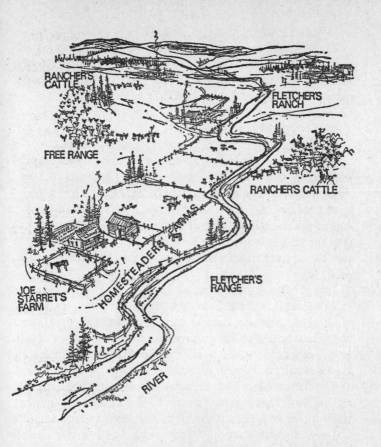

some money and use that money to keep a few head of cattle. Keep the herd fenced in and feed them well so that they get fat. The fatter they are, the more money you will get when you sell them.'

'That's true enough,' interrupted Shane.

'But lots of people don't understand that yet,' my father went on. 'Keep the cattle fenced in and they can't run around so much. And so they get fatter. I'm only starting and already I am making more money for each animal than Fletcher on the other side of the river.'

'Who's Fletcher?' asked Shane.

'He's the big rancher on the other side of the river,' answered father. 'He owns all the land there and it stretches for miles. He doesn't need all of that land. He hasn't enough cows to use all of it. But he won't sell any of his land to a homesteader. He doesn't want any fences on his land. He doesn't want any here either.'

My father stopped to take breath and then went on.

'Fletcher uses his land in a wasteful way. He doesn't need so much land, but he can't understand that. He thinks that we small ranchers are a nuisance and he wants us to leave. His cows used to graze on the land behind us as well as on his side of the river. But now our fences are up and it isn't so easy for his cattle to graze there. Also our fences shut off part of the river and his cattle can't get to the water so easily.'

'Yes, I can see that,' Shane said.

'What he is really afraid of,' went on my father, 'is that more of us homesteaders will come. And we'll keep on coming and take up more and more land. And some will want to settle on the other side of the river – on Fletcher's side. Then Fletcher will really be in trouble.'

That was the last I heard of their conversation because my mother found me and sent me off to bed. After I left, mother went out on to the porch to join them in their conversation.

I tried to hear what they were saying, but I soon fell asleep. Later I woke up again and heard mother and father talking in their bedroom. They were talking very quietly and I could just hear them.

'Wasn't it strange,' I heard my mother say, 'how Shane wouldn't talk about himself.'

'Strange?' my father asked.

'Yes,' my mother replied. 'Everything about him is strange. I have never met a man like him before.'

'He's a special kind of man we get here,' said my father. 'They only live where there's lots of space and lots of grass. A bad one is terribly dangerous. A good one is the best kind of man you can find.

'I like him,' my mother said seriously. 'He's so nice and polite and gentle. He's not like the other men I have met out here. But there's still something strange about him . . . I don't know what.'

'Something mysterious,' suggested my father.

'Yes mysterious – but also dangerous,' added my mother.

'He's dangerous all right,' father said in a thoughtful way.

And the last words I heard before I fell asleep came from my father.

'Yes, he's dangerous – but not to us. In fact, I don't think you ever had a safer man in the house.'

I fell asleep wondering what those strange words of my father could mean.

POINTS FOR UNDERSTANDING

1. What do these words mean?
   fence lines
   open range
   homesteader
   rancher
   settler
2. Why did Joe Starret think that it was important to keep the cattle fenced in?
3. Why did Joe think that Fletcher's way of keeping cattle was wasteful?
4. Why was Fletcher afraid of more and more settlers coming into the valley?
5. Bob's mother thought that Shane was a dangerous man. Did Bob's father agree with this?

3. Shane Becomes a Friend

The next morning, after we had eaten a good breakfast, my mother and father persuaded Shane to stay a little longer. They reminded him that it had been raining heavily during the night and that the roads would be wet and muddy. Shane agreed to stay for a little longer.

Some strange things happened that day which helped us to get to know Shane better. And also helped Shane to get to know us.

The first thing was that Shane made friends with my

mother. She asked him to speak about the ladies he had seen in the big towns. She wanted to know what kind of dresses and hats they were wearing. And he was able to tell her all about them. As I said before, he noticed everything he saw and could remember it.

He sat there and told her how the ladies in the big towns were dressed. He said they were wearing wide brimmed bonnets. The bonnets had lots of flowers on top and wide brims. The brims had holes in them and a scarf or handkerchief was passed through these holes and tied in a knot under the chin.

I thought that it was foolish for a man to sit and talk about ladies' clothes. But father listened and seemed to think that it was all right. But I don't think he thought it was very interesting. He wanted to talk about crops and cattle and farming. But he seemed to understand that it was good for my mother to talk about things like ladies' hats with Shane. It was not often that she got the chance to hear about such things.

Shane went on for some time telling her all about ladies' dresses and hats and this pleased mother very much. She now had no more doubt about Shane. Perhaps he was mysterious, even dangerous, but she had decided that she liked him.

The next thing was the arrival of Ledyard. Mr Ledyard was a travelling trader. He came round the farms every two months sellings things that could not be bought in our small town. He brought the things round on a cart and took orders for other things. He would bring these orders the next time he came. He always tried to get as high a price as possible and would even try to cheat the farmers.

The last time he had been at our farm, father had asked him to bring a new seven pronged cultivator. When he arrived in front of the house, he jumped off the cart and called to father.

Father went to meet him and Shane stayed by the porch leaning against the end post. Ledyard pulled the cover off the

cart and there on the cart was the bright, shiny, new cultivator.

'There you are,' said Ledyard, 'that's the best buy I've made on this journey.'

'Hm-m-m-m,' said father, 'you've brought what I wanted. But when you talk about a best buy, that always means a lot of money. How much does it cost?'

'Well——now,' Ledyard was slow in his reply, 'it cost more than I said when I was last here. You might think it a lot. But think how much easier your work will be. Even the boy here will be able to use it quite easily.'

As he said this, Ledyard smiled. He was trying to be friendly. But father interrupted him quickly.

'Answer my question. How much does it cost?' said father.

Ledyard was quick to reply this time.

'I'll make it as cheap as I can,' he said. 'I will only make a little money out of this sale. You're a good customer. I'll let you have it for a hundred and ten dollars.'

Suddenly there was an interruption. Shane's voice broke into their conversation. And he spoke quietly and clearly.

'Let you have it,' said Shane, repeating Ledyard's words. 'I'm sure he'll let you have it for a hundred and ten dollars. I saw one exactly the same in a store in Cheyenne. The price was sixty dollars.'

Ledyard looked closely and coldly at Shane who was still leaning against the post.

'Who asked you to speak?' Ledyard asked in a threatening way.

'No one did,' replied Shane. And he seemed to move away from father and Ledyard.

'Well,' said Ledyard, speaking again to my father and not looking at Shane, 'you are getting it cheap at a hundred and ten dollars.'

My father couldn't decide and this made Ledyard angry.

'What's wrong?' he asked my father. 'You surely don't

believe what this tramp says. Look at his clothes – look at his . . .'

Just then Ledyard turned to point to Shane. Shane had come forward and was standing looking at Ledyard. Ledyard had stopped what he was saying. There was a look of fear in his eyes.

I could see why. Shane was standing straight. His hands were held tightly at his side and he was staring at Ledyard. I felt cold suddenly as I felt the day before. I could almost smell Ledyard's fear.

Father raised his head in the air and interrupted them both.

'Yes, Ledyard, I believe this man,' he said quietly, but in a very determined way. 'He's my guest. He's here at my invitation. But that's not my real reason for believing him. I can understand men. And I know him. I'll believe anything he wants to say any day of the year.'

Father's head came down slightly and he continued.

'I will pay you eighty dollars,' he said to Ledyard. 'Sixty is the price in the store. Add ten and you can keep another ten dollars for yourself. That makes eighty.'

Ledyard stared down at his hands, rubbing them as if they were cold.

'Where's the money?' he said.

Father paid him the money. Ledyard helped father get the cultivator off the cart and then he drove off as quickly as he could.

POINTS FOR UNDERSTANDING

1. How did Shane make friends with Bob's mother?
2. Was Ledyard afraid of Shane?
3. Did Joe Starret believe what Shane said because Shane was his guest?

4. The Old Tree Stump

The thing that finally made Shane and Father real friends was the old tree stump in front of the corral gate. It was the one thing on our farm that was untidy. Its roots went right down into the earth and each root was as hard as stone. And it was big – it was huge. A very large number of people could have sat down round it for supper.

Father had been digging and cutting at it since we moved on to the farm. But it was obstinate. It refused to be moved easily.

When Ledyard left the farm, Shane had moved quietly away. He had gone to the woodshed, and suddenly we heard the fierce strokes of an axe. Shane was trying to get rid of his anger at Ledyard's words by attacking the old tree stump.

Father immediately understood what Shane was doing. He went and got the other axe. He chose a root on the opposite side from Shane. There they were cutting with all their strength.

It had become a battle. The old tree stump was the enemy and father and Shane were attacking it.

When they had cut through the first roots, they did not stop. They moved round to another root and, when that was cut through, they began to cut another. And as the time passed, they went on cutting.

About midday there was an interruption. Mother had listened to all that Shane had said about the hats the ladies were wearing in the big towns. She had spent the morning making one like them for herself. Now she came out of the house wearing this hat.

She had taken an old hat and fixed it as Shane had told her. She came out of the house and walked proudly up to the men. But father and Shane were too busy cutting and digging at the old tree stump. They did not notice her.

'Well,' she said, 'aren't you going to look at me?'

They both stopped and stared at her.

'Have I got it right?' she asked Shane. 'Is this the way to do it?'

'Yes, ma'am,' Shane replied. 'That's almost right. Only thing is that the ladies in town have bigger brims to their hats.' And he turned back to his root.

'Joe Starret,' said mother, 'aren't you even going to tell me if you like this hat?'

'Look, Marian,' said father, 'you know I like you. You're the prettiest lady I've ever seen whether you're wearing a hat or not. Now stop disturbing us. Can't you see we're busy.' And he turned back to his root.

'You can both stop now, anyway,' said mother very firmly. 'Dinner is ready and I won't wait for you.'

She walked back to the house in anger. We all followed her and ate our dinner in silence. Mother was angry during the meal, but when the two men went back to the tree stump, she seemed to forget her anger.

She asked me what had happened. She wanted to know why father and Shane were cutting the tree stump out of the ground. I tried to tell her about Ledyard and what he had said about Shane. She seemed to understand and started on her work in the kitchen. She was happy now and singing to herself as she worked.

It was late evening before the men finished their work on the tree stump. Father and Shane stopped cutting and father bent down and got his hands under the stump. He pulled and pulled with all his strength. The tree stump was moving.

It took them another hour of pulling and cutting under the stump. Mother was quite happy now and she came out to watch. The stump was in the air at one end now. Father and Shane gave one final pull and tore the stump out of the hole. It rolled down the slope and lay defeated with its roots up in the air.

POINTS FOR UNDERSTANDING

1. Why did Shane start cutting at the old tree stump?
2. What finally made Shane and Joe Starret close friends?

5. Shane Decides to Stay

The next morning, I was so tired with all the excitement of Shane's arrival that I slept very late. When I woke up, I lay in bed for some time thinking about Shane. He was a strange and mysterious man, but he was also exciting. Father and mother seemed much more lively with him in the house.

Suddenly I realized how late it was and jumped out of bed. I was afraid that our visitor might have gone without saying goodbye to me. I quickly dressed and went downstairs.

They were still sitting round the table. Father was smoking

his pipe and mother and Shane were drinking coffee. None of them were talking. They stared at me when I suddenly rushed into the room.

'My heavens,' said mother. 'What's the matter? Is there something wrong?'

'I thought Shane might have left without saying goodbye to me,' I answered honestly.

Shane shook his head, looking straight at me.

'I wouldn't forget you, Bob,' he said quietly. Then he turned to mother and said in a joking way. 'And I won't forget your cooking, ma'am. If lots of strangers begin to call on you at meal times, you'll know why. I will tell everybody I meet on my travels what a good cook you are.'

'Now, that's an idea,' said my father continuing the joke. 'We could turn the farm into a boarding-house.' Marian will fill people with her meals, and I'll fill my pockets with their money.'

We all smiled at the joke. We spent some time joking like that and then there was silence. We all looked at one another without saying anything.

Then Shane stood up. I knew he was going to ride away from us and I wanted very much to stop him. But it was father who stopped Shane going.

'You are always in a hurry to be moving,' he said to Shane. 'Sit down a moment. I have a question to ask you.'

Father was speaking very seriously. Shane looked at him for a moment and then sat down again.

Father looked straight at him. 'Are you running away because you have done something wrong?' he asked quietly.

Shane was silent for a moment and then looked father straight in the eyes. 'No,' he replied, 'I'm not running away for any reason like that.'

'Good,' said father leaning forward and speaking slowly and clearly. Then he went on. 'Now that you have seen my farm, you will know that I am not a rancher. I am a simple farmer. I will always have some cattle. But my main interest is having a farm. I want a farm where crops will grow and not a ranch where cattle run wild.'

Shane nodded as if he understood clearly.

'Now,' continued father, 'this farm isn't as big as it will be one day. But it is already too big for one man. There's enough work here for two men. I had a young man working for me. But you remember that I told you about Fletcher, the big rancher. Well, two of Fletcher's men began to argue with the young man. He was badly beaten up[8] and he left the valley in a hurry.'

'So Fletcher is trying to be a nuisance,' Shane interrupted. 'He wants to make it difficult for you to run this farm. He wants to make it difficult for you so that you will leave.'

Father looked very determined. 'Fletcher can try,' he said, 'but he won't find it easy to drive me away.[9] I've got a job to do here and it's too big for one man – even for me. Will you stay here and help me get things ready for the winter?'

Shane rose to his feet.

'I never thought that I would be a farmer, Starret. But you've got the help you need. I'll stay here and work for you. And your cooking, ma'am, will be all the wages I need.' As Shane said this, he turned to my mother and smiled.

Father slapped his hands on his knees to show that he was pleased. 'You'll get good wages and you'll work for them,' he said. 'Now why don't you get into town and get some work clothes. Go to Sam Grafton's shop and tell him that I will pay for the clothes.'

Shane was already at the door. 'I'll pay for my own clothes,' he said and was gone.

POINTS FOR UNDERSTANDING

1. Why was Bob afraid when he woke up late?
2. What question did Joe Starret want to ask Shane?
3. What happened to the cowboy who had been working for Joe Starret?

6. The Mystery of the Gun

After Shane went off, my mother spoke seriously to my father.

'Are you sure that you are doing the right thing, Joe Starret?' she asked. 'He doesn't look like a farmer to me. He's been used to plenty of money and a good life. You can tell that. He said himself that he doesn't know anything about farming.'

'Neither did I when I started,' replied my father. 'What a man knows isn't important. It's what he is that matters. Anything that Shane does will be done well. You watch.'

'Perhaps,' said mother, still doubtful.

'I am absolutely sure about Shane,' said father. 'He's certain to be useful to us. Did you notice how he was interested in Fletcher? Fletcher's men drove away the other helper, but they won't drive Shane away. That's why he wants to stay. He knows that I'm in trouble and he's not the kind of man who will leave me. Nobody will push him around or drive him away. He's the kind of man that I need.'

Shane's return interrupted the conversation. He came back with his work clothes and went into the barn where he was going to live. He came back ready for work.

Shane soon showed that he could work hard. He could work as hard as father. But he made me feel that he was not really a farmer. There was still something different about him. He learned quickly and was not proud. He would do the dirtiest jobs on the farm willingly and well. He was always ready to take the most difficult part of any job. But still I felt that farming was not, and never would be, his real job.

I think father was right. The work on the farm was not the real reason for Shane staying. It was Fletcher. If Fletcher tried any tricks, Shane would be ready.

His readiness and alertness became clear at our next meal.

At that meal he did something strange which we could not understand at first.

For as long as I remember, father had always sat in the big chair at the end of the table. I felt that chair belonged to my father. When Shane came into supper that evening, he stood beside that chair and waited for us all to sit down. Father sat down on another chair and Shane sat down on the chair that had always been father's.

We were surprised at this. And Mother looked rather angry.

Later we saw why Shane had done this. One of our neighbours came to visit us. He knocked at the door, and opened it and came straight into the room where we were sitting. Our neighbours often did this. But as he did so, the first person who could see him was Shane. Shane had chosen that seat so that he would be directly in front of anyone who came in the door.

Shane was protecting us. And it was like that all the time. When he sat on the porch, he sat with his back to the wall. He liked to be able to see everything that was happening in front of him.

It was two weeks later that I suddenly noticed the strangest thing of all about Shane. I don't know why I did not notice it earlier. But when I noticed it, it surprised me more than anything else. Shane did not carry a gun.

In those days guns were as common as boots and saddles. Everybody carried a gun. In our valley they were used for hunting animals. But Shane never carried a gun. And even more mysterious was the fact that he had one.

I discovered his gun by accident. One day I went into the barn where he slept. His saddle-roll was lying on his bed. The same saddle-roll that Shane had not let me touch on his first day here. This was unusual because he always put it away under his bed. He must have forgotten it this time because it was lying on his pillow.

I felt very curious and reached out to touch it. I felt a gun inside the saddle-roll. My curiosity was too strong and I was too young to realize that I was doing wrong. I untied the straps of the saddle-roll and took out the gun. It was the most beautiful pistol that I had ever seen.

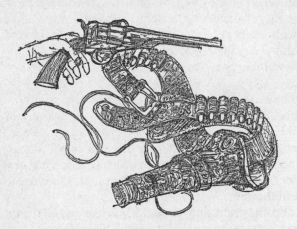

I put my hand on the pistol and pulled it out of the holster. It came out so easily that I could not believe that it was there in my hand. It was heavy like my father's but much easier to handle. When I held it up and pretended to take aim,[10] it seemed to balance itself in my hand.

Ths pistol was clean and polished. I knew that Shane loved that gun. It was so well looked after and it was so beautiful. But why did he not wear it? What a strange mystery this was! Anyone who owned a gun like that would be proud to wear it. If it was mine, I would wear it night and day. I could not understand why Shane kept it hidden away.

Carefully I put the pistol back in the holster. I tied up the saddle-roll and left it on the pillow.

I ran out of the barn and down to the corral where father was working.

'Father,' I said excitedly, 'do you know what Shane has in his saddle-roll?'

'Probably a gun,' replied father.

'But how did you know?' I asked. 'Have you seen it?'

'No,' replied father, 'but I thought that's what he would have.'

I was extremely surprised. 'Well, why doesn't he ever wear it?' I asked. 'Do you think it's because he can't use it very well?'

Father laughed at this. 'He can probably use it better than any man alive,' he replied.

'Then why doesn't he wear it?' I repeated. 'Why don't you ask him why he doesn't wear it?'

Father looked straight at me very seriously. 'Bob,' he said, 'that's one question I'll never ask Shane. And don't you say anything about it to him. His gun is his own private business. I'm sure that he has some special reason of his own for not wearing his gun. But if he wants to keep it private, we must respect him and not ask him anything about it.'

I was still curious. I was too young to understand how grown men think and act.

As I stood in silence, my father put his hand on my shoulder. 'Bob,' he said, 'listen to me. Don't get too fond of[11] Shane.'

This remark of my father's surprised me even more than the mystery of the gun.

'Why not?' I asked. 'Is there something wrong with him?'

'No-o-o-o,' replied father, hesitating as he spoke. 'There's nothing wrong with Shane. There's more right about him than almost any man you'll ever meet. But . . .' he hesitated again. 'But he's not going to stay here for ever. I'm sure of that. He'll be going away one day and then you'll be upset if you get too fond of him.'

I felt there was another reason for father warning me about growing fond of Shane. Perhaps it was because of the gun. But father did not want to speak about it. So I did not ask any more questions.

1. What was Shane's real reason for staying on the farm?
2. Why did Shane sit in the chair that had always been used by Bob's father?
3. How did Bob discover that Shane had a gun?
4. Was Bob's father surprised to learn that Shane had a gun?
5. Did Joe Starret ask Shane why he did not wear his gun?
6. Why did Joe Starret warn his son not to get too fond of Shane?

7. Fletcher Comes Back

I think that was the happiest summer of my life.

There was no trouble in our valley. Fletcher was away on business most of the summer. He was trying to get a contract[12] to sell large amounts of beef to an Indian Reservation some distance away.

His men were still in the valley. But they kept to the other side of the river and did not trouble us at all. Some of them were even friendly. It was Fletcher who made them do things that troubled the homesteaders. Fletcher wanted us to go away and used his men to make life difficult for us. Now that Fletcher was away, they left us in peace.

Before Shane came, I had admired Fletcher's cowboys. They had been my heroes. I had wanted to dress like them and ride like them. Now Shane was my hero. And my father, also, of course. He was very, very special. In my eyes there was no other person like him. I wanted to be exactly like my father when I grew up.

During those long summer months father and Shane worked together on the farm. They finished more work in those few months than father thought he would finish in two years. Mother worked in the house making clothes and preparing food for the winter. Sometimes I helped mother, but I liked to work with Shane and father.

It was the happiest summer of my life.

Then everything changed. The summer was over. It was autumn and school began again. The days were growing shorter and it began to get colder. In the early morning I ran most of the way to school to get warm. Winter was approaching.

But more than summer was over. Fletcher had come back. He had got his contract to sell beef to the Indians. Now he wanted all the land he could get for his cattle. He was more determined than ever to make us leave the valley.

The friendliness which had grown in the warm days of summer was now dying away in the first cold days of autumn.

Fletcher was often in town. He talked to people about his need for more land. He was saying that now he needed the whole range on both sides of the river. And he said that he wanted to buy the homesteaders' farms.

Fletcher was saying that he would pay a fair price,[13] but we knew what he meant. Ledyard, the trader who came every now and again, tried to cheat the homesteaders. But Fletcher's cheating would be much worse than Ledyard's. Fletcher would pay less than half the price of a farm if he could.

A person who did not know our small town might be curious. He might wonder why the homesteaders were worried. And he might think they were worried about nothing. The homesteaders had bought their land from the government and had paid for it. How could Fletcher force anyone to leave?

The answer to this question is simple. The government was hundreds of miles away in Washington. The nearest marshal[14] was one hundred miles away. And we did not even have a sheriff[15] in the town.

There had never been any reason for having a sheriff. The town was very small. In fact it was not really a town at all. It was just a few houses and stores by the roadside. There was the school which the men of the town had built not long ago. And it was a building with just one room. That was the school that I went to. And the biggest building in the town was Sam Grafton's store.

If there was going to be trouble, the homesteaders would have to fight for themselves. They could not hope for help from the government or from the law.

There were three main groups of people where we lived. Fletcher and his cowboys formed one group. The homesteaders with their small fenced-in farms formed another. And then the third group was the people who lived and worked in the town.

This third group was important. Fletcher would find it difficult to drive us away if the townspeople supported the homesteaders. Unfortunately, Fletcher was the richest and most important man in the valley. He now had his contract and a contract meant money and work, both for his cowboys and for the townspeople too. The townspeople would probably support Fletcher if he decided to make trouble for us homesteaders. And now Fletcher was talking in town of his need for more land. It seemed certain that he was going to make trouble.

My father was sure that the town would grow bigger in the future. He was certain that more and more settlers would come to the valley. This would bring money and work to the town. But that was in the future. For the moment it was Fletcher who had the money and the work. The townspeople knew that and respected him.

Sam Grafton was an important man in the town. The townspeople thought of him as their real leader. He owned the shop where Shane had bought his clothes. In the same building as the shop, Sam Grafton owned a saloon where people went to sit and relax and play cards.

Sam Grafton was a real businessman. He never spoke about the difference between Fletcher and us homesteaders. He sold things to Fletcher's men and to the homesteaders. Both Fletcher's men and the homesteaders often went into Grafton's saloon to have a drink or play cards. Sam did not support one side more than the other. He treated them equally and his business did well.

That's why it was only natural that the trouble should start in Sam Grafton's saloon. It was the one place in town where the homesteaders met Fletcher's cowboys.

POINTS FOR UNDERSTANDING

1. Why was Fletcher away most of the summer?
2. Why did Fletcher want more space for his cattle?
3. Would Fletcher really pay a fair price for a farm?
4. How could Fletcher force the homesteaders to leave?
5. Why was the support of the townspeople so important to the homesteaders?
6. Why did the townspeople respect Fletcher?
7. Why was Sam Grafton's saloon an important place in the town?

8. Is Shane Afraid?

When Fletcher returned, he soon heard about Shane. Both the townspeople and the homesteaders were curious about Shane. They wondered who he was and where he had come from. And most of them thought that Shane was dangerous.

During the summer Shane had often talked to us. He talked most of all to father when he was working beside him on the farm. But he always talked about general things. He never talked about himself or about his past life. We did not know any more about Shane after those months than we had known on the first day.

The other boys at school often questioned me about Shane. I knew that father did not want me to say anything. So I pretended that I did not know what they were talking about.

Fletcher soon heard about Shane and decided that Shane was his real enemy. Fletcher had succeeded in driving away the other cowboy who had worked for father on our farm. I knew why this cowboy had left because I saw him the night he came back from town. He had been beaten by Fletcher's men. He came back badly beaten up. He had packed his bags and had left our farm immediately.

Now Fletcher knew that he must drive Shane away also. And everyone else knew that too. The curiosity of the townspeople and the homesteaders became even greater than before. But there was a difference. Now they did not want to know about Shane's past. They were now interested in his future. They wanted to know what Shane would do when Fletcher tried to drive him away.

They did not have long to wait. After Fletcher had been back about a week, his men began to find more and more work near our farm. They were obviously watching us and trying to get a close look at Shane. At all times of the day there was one of Fletcher's men near our farm. Sometimes his men were on the other side of the river from where they could see our farm clearly. Sometimes they came on our side of the river and went past right in front of the corral.

Then one afternoon the trouble started. The cause of the trouble was a broken spade. Shane was digging and the spade broke while he was working with it. It was the metal part of the spade that broke and it would have to be mended at the blacksmiths.

'It will have to be mended in town,' said father, who was working beside him.

Shane stared out over the river. One of Fletcher's cowboys was riding lazily up and down. He was obviously watching us.

'I'll take the spade into town,' said Shane.

Father looked at Shane and then he looked across the river. He saw what Shane had noticed and he smiled.

'All right,' he said. It's as good a time as any to begin the fight. Just wait a minute and I'll be ready to come with you.' Father walked towards the house.

'Wait a moment, Joe,' said Shane. His voice was gentle but it made father stop.

'I said that *I'll* take the spade into town,' Shane continued, 'and I mean by myself.'

'What,' said my father, 'do you think I would let you go alone? They will be waiting for you in town. Suppose they try to . . .'

And then father stopped. He had noticed the cold, determined look on Shane's face. And he saw the way Shane was standing. It was the same Shane that had put fear into Ledyard.

'I'm sorry,' said father, 'I should know you better by now. You're the kind of man who must do things alone.'

Father watched in silence while Shane jumped up into the seat of the wagon.

I wanted to go but I was afraid that father would stop me. I waited until Shane had driven the wagon out into the lane. Then I ran round behind the corral and out on to the lane. I jumped on to the back of the wagon as it went past.

As I did so, I noticed the cowboy on the other side of the river. He turned his horse and rode off towards Fletcher's ranch-house.

He was certainly going to tell Fletcher that Shane was on his way into town.

Shane also saw the cowboy moving away and that seemed to amuse him. He reached back and helped me on to the wagon seat beside him. I was afraid that he might send me home.

Instead he said to me with a smile: 'I'll buy you a knife when we get into town.'

And he did buy me a knife. First we went to the blacksmith. The blacksmith said that it would take about an hour to mend the spade. After that he took me to a store and bought me a knife. It was a beautiful knife. Then we went to Grafton's.

I sat on the porch outside and cut away at a piece of wood with my new knife. Shane went through Grafton's store and into the saloon for a drink.

A few moments later, two cowboys came galloping down

the road. They slowed down when they came to Grafton's and got off their horses in front of the shop. They were both Fletcher's men.

I had seen one of them before. His name was Chris. He was a young man of about twenty-two years old. Chris had worked with Fletcher for several years. He was well known for his cheerful manner and his courage. I did not know the other man. He was a little older than Chris and he looked hard and tough. He must have been one of the new men that Fletcher had brought into the valley when he came back with his contract.

They paid no attention to me. They stepped softly up on to the porch. Then they went over to the window and looked into the saloon. Chris pointed to someone inside. The new man stiffened. He moved closer for a better look. Suddenly he turned round and walked right past me to his horse.

Chris was surprised and hurried after him. Neither of them noticed me.

'What's wrong?' said Chris as the other man got on his horse.

'I'm leaving,' said the other cowboy.

'But what's wrong? I don't understand you,' said Chris.

'I'm leaving now and I'm going away for ever,' replied the man turning his horse towards the road.

'What's wrong?' repeated Chris still surprised. 'Do you know that man in there? Have you met him before?'

'I am not saying that I know him,' replied the man. 'What I am saying is that I am not staying here any longer. I am leaving now. And you can tell Fletcher that I don't like this place anyway.'

'You're afraid! That's what is wrong,' shouted Chris as the other man started to move away.

For a moment the man turned round and looked really angry. Then he said, 'All right, you can say that I'm afraid if you like.' And with those words he turned his back on Chris and galloped off.

Chris stood still for a moment in amazement. Then he shook his head and said out loud so that I could hear, 'It doesn't make any difference. I'll fight him myself.' And he walked straight up on to the porch and into the saloon.

POINTS FOR UNDERSTANDING

1. What had Fletcher's men done to the cowboy who had worked for Joe Starret?
2. Why was there always one of Fletcher's men near Joe Starret's farm?
3. Two cowboys followed Shane to Grafton's saloon. Chris stayed but what did the other cowboy do when he saw Shane through the window?
4. What did Chris decide to do?

9. Pigs and Soda Pop

From the way that Chris and the other cowboy had been speaking, I knew that they were speaking about Shane. I rushed up on to the porch and went into Grafton's behind Chris. I went over to the opening that led into the saloon. I climbed up on to a box that stood beside the wall. From the top of the box I could see most of the inside of the saloon. Also I could hear quite clearly what anyone said.

Shane was standing beside the bar quite relaxed. In one hand he had a drink and his other hand was on top of the bar. Chris came up to about six feet away from Shane and ordered a whiskey.

Whiskey was the most common drink in those days. And it was a man's drink. If a man drank something else, like a soda pop for example, the other men would have said that he was weak. Whiskey was a strong man's drink.

I saw Shane looking closely at Chris but in a way that Chris did not notice. And I thought that Shane looked disappointed. Perhaps he was thinking that Chris looked too easy to beat in a fight.

Chris waited until Shane got his whiskey and drank some of it. Then he turned to Shane and looked at him as if he had just seen him for the first time.

'Hello, farmer,' said Chris. And he said it in a way that showed that he did not like farmers.

Shane looked straight at him. 'Speaking to me?' he asked quietly and finished his drink.

'Why!' said Chris as if surprised, 'you're drinking whiskey. That's a man's drink. It's not a drink for farmers.'

Chris turned round to the other men in the saloon. 'Do you see that?' he said. 'This farmer drinks whiskey. I didn't think that these dirty farmers drank anything stronger than soda pop.' Chris began to laugh but stopped when he realized that everyone else was silent.

'Some of us do,' replied Shane quite friendly. Then he was suddenly no longer friendly and his voice turned as cold as ice. 'You've had your fun. Now go back to Fletcher and tell him to send a grown-up man next time.' He turned away and shouted to Will Atkey, the barman, 'Do you have any soda pop? I'd like a bottle.'

Will hesitated, looking rather surprised. Then he ran past me into the store room where Mr Grafton kept soda pop for us school children.

Chris stood quiet. I think he was wondering what Shane was planning to do. Then he deliberately looked round the room and began to sniff as if he smelled a bad smell.

'Hey, Will,' he called. 'What's been happening in here? There's a bad smell.' He stared at Shane. 'You, farmer,' he said, 'what kind of animals have you and Starret got at that place up there? Pigs?'

As Chris said this, Shane was just taking hold of the bottle of soda pop that Will Atkey had brought him. The top of his fingers turned white as he held the bottle very tightly. I was surprised that the bottle did not break.

Shane moved slowly to turn round and face Chris. He was staring straight at Chris and his eyes flashed with fire. Every part of his body stiffened and he looked like an animal ready to jump.

There was complete silence in the room. Everyone looked at the two men facing one another. Chris and Shane stood for a few moments in silence. Shane's face looked hard and cold.

Then Shane suddenly relaxed. He looked up over Chris's head, out through the store and towards the hills in the distance. Still holding the bottle of soda pop, Shane walked quietly past Chris as if he did not see him. He went out through the store and on to the road and walked away.

Chris looked very proud and pleased with himself. He really believed that Shane had walked out because he was afraid of him. 'You saw that,' he called to Will who was standing behind the bar. 'He walked out on me.'

Chris pushed his hat to the back of his head and laughed loudly. 'And he went out with his bottle of soda pop!' said Chris, laughing. He was still laughing as he got on his horse and rode back to Fletcher's.

'That boy, Chris, is a fool,' Mr Grafton said after Chris had gone out of the store.

Will Atkey came over to Mr Grafton. 'I never thought that Shane would have walked away from a fight,' he said.

'He was afraid, Will,' said Sam Grafton.

'Yes,' replied Will, 'That's what is so strange. I did not think that Shane would have been afraid of Chris.'

Mr Grafton looked at Will as if he thought him rather stupid. 'No, Will,' he said, 'you haven't understood me. Shane wasn't afraid of Chris. He was afraid of himself.'

Mr Grafton looked thoughtful and also rather sad. 'There's trouble coming,' he said half to Will and half to himself. 'The worst trouble we have ever had.'

POINTS FOR UNDERSTANDING

1. Explain the importance of the following expressions:
   soda pop
   pigs
   this farmer drinks whiskey
2. What did Will Atkey think was the reason for Shane refusing to fight?
3. What was Shane's real reason for refusing to fight?

10. Shane Decides to Fight

The other people in the saloon were like Will Atkey. They did not understand why Shane had walked out. They thought that Shane was afraid to fight Chris. Only Mr Grafton and myself understood the real reason.

And father understood too. When we got back to the farm, father asked Shane what had happened.

'Did you meet any cowboys in town?' said father.

'One of Fletcher's boys followed me into town to say hello,' replied Shane.

'No, you're wrong,' I interrupted. 'There were two of them.' And as I said this, I felt proud. I had seen something that Shane had not noticed.

'Two?' asked Shane in surprise. 'What did the other one do?'

'He went up to the window,' I replied. 'He looked in and Chris pointed someone out to him. It must have been you. He looked in and saw you. When he saw you clearly, he left Chris standing by the window. He turned round, walked to his horse, jumped on it and rode off.'

'Back to Fletcher's ranch?' asked Shane.

'No,' I replied, 'he rode off in the opposite direction. And he shouted to Chris that he was never coming back again.'

Father and Shane looked at one another. Father was smiling.

'You frightened one away,' he said, 'and you didn't even know it. And what about Chris? What did you do to him?'

'Nothing,' replied Shane. 'He said a few rude words and then I went back to the blacksmith's shop.'

Father did not ask any more questions. He immediately understood why Shane had not fought Chris.

'It's a pity,' said father, 'that the other man rode off. If he had stayed, you could have fought them both. Then it would have been a fair fight.'

Shane looked very thoughtful. 'It's a pity in another way,' he said. 'Perhaps Chris won't understand why I walked away.'

And he was right. Chris thought that Shane had been afraid of him. He told Fletcher this and the news spread all round the valley. Fletcher's men told everybody and people believed what they said. The other people who had been in the saloon at the time told the same story.

Only Mr Grafton and myself and father knew the real reason. Shane had been afraid of himself. He had not wanted to hurt Chris.

Things began to get worse. Fletcher's cowboys began to come past our farm every day and say rude words to us.

'What a bad smell,' one of them would say loud enough for us to hear. 'It must be those pigs.' And they would all laugh.

And they were rude to the other homesteaders too. They were rude to them whenever they could be. If a homesteader went into Grafton's, someone would shout out: 'Here's another one who wants a bottle of soda pop.' And everyone in the saloon would join in the laughter.

Even the townspeople began to laugh with Fletcher's men against the homesteaders. They had treated the homesteaders and Fletcher's men equally before. Now they began to think that all the homesteaders were weak men. Only Mr Grafton was silent and kept his opinion to himself.

At first Shane and father were not worried. They knew the truth and were content to let other people think what they wanted to think.

After a few days, however, father started to worry. He saw how the story about Shane was worrying the other homesteaders. The homesteaders believed that Chris was telling the truth. Perhaps Shane was not so strong after all. Perhaps he had been afraid to fight Chris. They were also becoming more and more angry. Every day they had to listen to rude words about pigs and soda pop.

The homesteaders' friendliness to father and to Shane began to change. If Shane had fought Chris in the saloon, then the insults about pigs and soda pop would never have started. They believed that the insults were Shane's fault. Before, they had thought of father as their leader. Now, because father was connected with Shane, the homesteaders were beginning to lose their respect for father.

Shane soon noticed this change of attitude to father. And I think it was this more than anything else that forced Shane to do something.

One evening two of the homesteaders came to see father. The first was Ernie Wright. He had the last farm up the valley. Ernie's farm was nearest to Fletcher's range on our side of the river. Ernie was a strong man and could fight. But he was lazy. He would often go off hunting when he should have been working on his farm. Also, because his farm was the nearest to Fletcher's range, he suffered most from the rudeness.

The other homesteader who came with Ernie Wright that evening was Henry Shipstead. Shipstead was a good farmer but he was not a fighting man. If Fletcher made life too difficult for him, he would sell his farm and go away.

Ernie Wright and Henry Shipstead went into the kitchen and began to talk with father. Shane was sitting alone on the porch outside. From where he was sitting, Shane could easily hear what they were saying in the kitchen.

Ernie Wright was complaining about the insults. 'I can't take much more,' he was saying. 'Fletcher's cowboys are always asking me about my pigs. They know there isn't a pig in any farm in the valley. But they keep on talking about the smell and asking me how my pigs are doing.'

Father did not think the insult about pigs was very important. He started to laugh at what Ernie was saying and this made Ernie very angry.

'It isn't something to laugh about,' said Ernie bitterly. 'Chris was in Grafton's saloon last evening. He was saying that Shane must be a very thirsty man now that he is too afraid to come in for his soda pop.'

Wright joined in the argument. 'You can't escape it, Joe,' he said to my father. 'Your man is responsible for all these insults about pigs and soda pop. Chris insulted Shane and offered to fight him. Shane refused and walked out. The insults are all Shane's fault.'

'You know what Fletcher is trying to do,' said Henry Shipstead. 'He is trying to make us homesteaders angry with these insults. Soon one of us will lose his temper[16] and start a fight. Fletcher's cowboys are waiting for this. They will beat up the first homesteader who starts a fight and make him leave the valley. That will be the beginning of the end.'

'And it will probably be me,' said Ernie. 'I have had enough of their insults. I know it will be foolish, but . . .'

Father stopped Ernie speaking. 'Listen,' he said, 'What's that?'

It was the sound of a horse galloping off down the lane. Father rushed to the door. The others were closely behind him.

'Is it Shane?' asked Ernie Wright and Henry Shipstead together.

Father nodded, 'Yes, it's Shane. He has gone off to town. Now all we can do is wait and see what happens.'

POINTS FOR UNDERSTANDING

1. Try to answer the following questions without looking back in your book. When you have answered them, you can look back to see if you have given the correct answers.

'If he had stayed, you could have fought them both. Then it would have been a fair fight.'
(a) Who said these words?
(b) 'If he'. Who is the 'he' here?
(c) 'you could'. Who is the 'you'?
(d) 'them both'. Who are the two men in 'them both'?
(e) Why would it have been a fair fight if 'he' had stayed?

2. What did Chris tell Fletcher?
3. What did everyone in the valley begin to believe about Shane?
4. What effect did the insults of Fletcher's men have on the other homesteaders?
5. What did Shane do when he heard Ernie and Henry speaking to Bob's father?

11. Chris Against Shane

We sat together silently in the house and waited. Mother came in from the bedroom. She had heard all that had been said and knew what was going on. She made a pot of coffee and we all sat down and drank coffee and waited for Shane to return.

Twenty minutes later we heard a horse coming very fast up the lane. It came to a stop outside the house. There were quick steps on the porch and Shane suddenly stood in the doorway. He was breathing strongly and his face was hard. His mouth was pulled tightly into a hard line and his eyes were deep and dark.

'Your pigs are dead and buried. No one will ever speak about them again,' Shane said, looking bitterly at Wright and Shipstead. He was bitter with them because they had made him go and fight Chris.

Then he turned to father and his face softened, but his voice was still bitter. He was very unhappy about what he had done.

'That's another one finished,' he said to father. 'Chris won't be troubling anyone for a long time.'

He turned away and disappeared. We heard him leading his horse into the barn. Shane did not come back.

We had only a few moments to wait before we heard all

about what had happened. Ed Howells, another of the homesteaders, came running into the house. Wright and Shipstead looked rather ashamed, but they wanted to know what had happened.

'Where's Shane?' Ed asked.

'Out in the barn,' replied father.

'Did he tell you what happened?' asked Ed.

'He said something about the pigs being dead and buried,' replied father.

'Yes,' said Ed very excitedly, 'Fletcher's men won't say anything about pigs any more. And they won't say anything about soda pop either. I never saw anything like it in my life.'

With those words Ed sat down in a chair. He was so excited that we had to wait a few moments before he could tell his story. Then Ed told us what had happened.

Ed was in Grafton's store buying some things when Shane came in. Chris and Red Marlin, another of Fletcher's cowboys, were in the saloon playing cards. Shane walked in quietly. But the moment he walked in, everyone in the saloon stopped talking. There was complete silence.

It was easy to see why. Shane looked cool and relaxed. But he moved in a way that made him seem like a dangerous man. Neither Chris nor Red Marlin said anything about pigs or soda. They both knew that this was not the time for insults.

Shane went up to the bar.

'Two bottles of soda pop,' he called out to Will Atkey.

When Will brought the bottles of soda pop, Shane took one of them and turned to Chris.

'I've bought you a drink,' Shane said quite simply and put the bottle of soda pop on the table in front of Chris.

For a few seconds there was absolute silence in the saloon. You could have heard a fly crawling on the window pane.

Chris looked carefully at Shane. Then he suddenly picked up the bottle and threw it at Shane's head.

44

Shane ducked[17] and the bottle went flying over his head. Then Shane moved so fast that he had caught Chris by the neck before the bottle hit the ground. Shane pulled Chris out of his chair and on to the table.

As Chris tried to escape, Shane suddenly let go of his neck and hit him three times on the face. He hit him fiercely and hard.

Shane stepped back. Chris shook his head so that he could see straight. Then he faced Shane and came towards him. Chris was certainly brave, but Shane was clever. Shane let Chris come towards him. Chris's fists were moving towards Shane's face.

Shane ducked again and came in under Chris's fists. He punched Chris hard in the stomach. As Chris bent down in pain, Shane brought his fist up and hit Chris hard on the mouth and nose.

Chris staggered[18] back and nearly fell. His lips were smashed and blood was pouring from his nose. But Chris was still brave. He stood up and came running once again towards Shane. His fists were flying wildly in the air.

Shane ducked once more and moved quickly to one side. As Chris went past him, Shane caught one of his arms. Shane held it tightly and twisted it fiercely. There was a loud crack. Chris screamed with pain as Shane lifted him in the air by the broken arm and threw him across the room on to the floor.

Chris lay still on the floor. His broken arm was twisted behind him. He would not fight again for a long time.

Shane did not look at Chris. He stood straight and still. Every part of his body looked alive and alert, but he stood completely still. Only his eyes moved. He looked slowly round the room until his eyes found Red Marlin.

Shane's eyes stopped moving. He stared straight at Red. Red seemed to become smaller and did not move from his chair.

Shane spoke to Red Marlin. 'Perhaps,' he said very softly. But Shane's soft voice made everyone in the saloon shake with fear. 'Perhaps you have something to say about soda pop or about pigs.'

Red Marlin sat so quietly that it looked as if he was not breathing. Small drops of sweat appeared on his face. He was afraid. He was terribly afraid. The other people in the saloon knew Red was afraid but they did not blame him. They had all seen what Shane had done to Chris.

Then Shane changed again. The hardness left him and he relaxed. He went over to Chris and gently lifted him on to a

46

table. Shane took a wet cloth from the bar and carefully wiped the blood from Chris's face.

Shane spoke and his voice rang across the room at Red Marlin. 'Take him home,' he said, 'and get his arm fixed. Take good care of him. He is a brave man.'

Then he seemed to forget everyone else in the room and he spoke to Chris as if that unconscious[19] figure could hear him.

'There's only one thing wrong with you,' he said, 'you are young. That's the one thing that time can change.'

Then Shane was out of the room and away.

We all listened in absolute silence while Ed Howells was describing the fight. When I heard how Shane had beaten Chris, I wanted to jump up and down with excitement. Ernie Wright and Henry Shipstead looked amazed and pleased too. They now knew that Shane was not afraid.

'I think that Shane is the most dangerous man I have ever seen,' said Ed Howells at the end of his story. I am very glad that he is working for Joe Starret here and not for Fletcher!'

Father looked triumphantly at Ernie Wright and Henry Shipstead.

'What do you think now?' he asked them. 'Do you still think that I've made a mistake?'

Before either of them could say anything, mother suddenly interrupted.

'Joe Starret,' she said. You've made a bad mistake.'

We were all surprised. What could mother mean? Father looked at her. He did not understand what she meant.

'What do you mean, Marian?' he asked.

'Look what you've done,' she replied. 'You asked Shane to stay and now look what has happened. I am worried about what this fighting will do to him. I feel that Shane has been happy here with us this summer. He felt he had escaped from fighting and hurting people. Now what will happen to him? I'm sure he will change and change for the worse.'

I don't think that the others knew what mother was talking about. Ed Howells and Ernie Wright and Henry Shipstead soon said goodbye and hurried off. They wanted to tell the other homesteaders about Shane's victory. Father looked thoughtful but did not say anything more. Soon we all went to bed.

I lay in bed thinking. I felt that I understood what mother was trying to say. Shane had been a fighter all his life. We did not know where he had come from. We knew nothing about his past life. I still did not understand the mystery of the beautiful pistol in his saddle roll. But I felt that mother was right. Shane had been a fighting man all his life. Now he felt that he had had enough of fighting and he wanted to escape from it.

He had been happy living with us. He had changed quite a lot during the summer months. But now he was back again to fighting. And as I fell asleep, I wondered if Shane would change again.

After a few days it turned out that mother was right. Shane was a changed man. He tried to pretend that nothing had changed. But I noticed the difference. He was no longer happy. He did not talk nearly so much. He often wandered round the farm by himself. He could not work at any job for a long time. He no longer felt calm and relaxed.

POINTS FOR UNDERSTANDING

1. What did Shane mean when he said: 'Your pigs are dead and buried'?
2. Shane bought two bottles of soda pop. What did he do with one of them?
3. Why would Chris not fight again for a long time?
4. What did Shane say was the one thing that was wrong with Chris?
5. In what ways did Shane change after the fight?

48

12. Five Against One

After the night Shane beat up Chris in the saloon, there was peace again in the valley. Fletcher's cowboys kept away from the homesteaders' farms. There were no more insults about pigs or about soda pop.

Fletcher's men were busy anyway on the other side of the river. They were building a big, new corral. Fletcher was planning to drive all his cattle into this corral in the spring. He had to do this to keep his contract with the Indians. We sometimes saw a cowboy riding on the other side of the river, but they did not come near to our farm.

Fletcher's men did not come near us now, but father and Shane were more watchful than ever. They were both on the alert and ready for any trouble. The two of them always worked together now. They did not separate to do jobs on different parts of the farm. They stayed together all the time. And if we needed anything from the stores, they would ride into town together.

And father started to wear his pistol all the time. He even wore it when he was working in the fields. He started to wear it on the morning after Shane's fight with Chris.

I saw him looking at Shane as he put the belt round his waist. He was obviously asking Shane if he was going to wear his gun. But Shane shook his head. Father nodded to show that he understood. He saw that Shane did not want to wear his gun and they went out to the field together without saying a word.

Now the weather was beautiful. It was autumn and the nights were cold. But during the day the weather was wonderful. In fact the days were so fine that I started to escape from school. No one could expect a healthy young boy to stay shut up in a school room in such beautiful weather. I used to slip away with another boy during the lunch break. We often went down to the river to fish or to swim.

49

And it was this escaping of mine that led to Shane being separated from father. And it brought Shane a lot of trouble. This is how it happened.

Every Saturday we all went into town to get the things that we needed for the house and the farm. We all went together, mother and father and Shane and myself. We always called in at Sam Grafton's store. Sam Grafton's daughter was the school teacher. Her name was Jane Grafton. And Jane Grafton had asked mother to come and see her.

Miss Grafton wanted to tell mother about my escaping. She wanted mother to punish me. She had asked mother in the note to come and see her when mother was in the store on Saturday.

This Saturday, mother bought all the things that she needed and we put them on to the wagon. Then she spoke to father.

'I think you should come with me, Joe,' she said. 'That boy is getting too big for me to look after by myself.'

Father looked at Shane who was reading a newspaper.

'This won't take long,' he said. 'We'll be back in a moment.'

Shane nodded in agreement and mother and father went through another door which led into Miss Grafton's rooms. Shane folded his newspaper and walked slowly through the store into the saloon. He looked round the room carefully and walked up to the bar. I followed Shane up to the saloon entrance. But I stopped there because I was not allowed to go into the saloon. I was not old enough to go inside. I stood at the opening which led into the saloon and waited there.

Shane ordered a drink and stood by the bar still alert and watchful. He was ready to be friendly with anyone who was ready to be friendly with him. But he was also ready to be unfriendly with anyone who was unfriendly to him.

Then I suddenly saw Red Marlin come into the store and look through into the saloon. Shane saw him also, but Shane could not see what I saw. There were another four cowboys coming behind Red and one of them was Morgan.

Morgan was Fletcher's foreman. He was the man in charge of Fletcher's cowboys and he made sure they did their work properly. Morgan was big and tough and today he looked very bitter and determined.

Although I was not allowed to go into the bar, I felt that I must help Shane. I ran straight into the saloon and up to Shane.

'Shane,' I whispered, 'there's another four with Marlin.'

But I was too late. Red Marlin was inside the saloon and Morgan and the others were coming in behind him.

There was another door at the back of the saloon. I pulled at Shane's trouser leg because I wanted him to escape through that door.

'Bobby, boy,' he said, 'do you want me to run away?'

Then I really knew how brave Shane was. He was my hero more than ever.

'This is going to be dangerous, Bob,' he said. 'Get out of here quick!'

I ran back to the entrance of the saloon and turned round to watch what was happening. I was so excited that I forgot to run and tell father. I just stood there as if my feet were tied to the floor.

Morgan was in front now with his men coming behind him. There was Red Marlin and another cowboy called Curly who was a friend of Chris. The other two were new men. I did not know them.

Morgan came about half way through the saloon towards Shane. Then he stopped. Shane and Morgan looked at one another. The other people in the saloon got up from the tables and stood back against the wall. Some even got out and left by the front doors. They knew there was going to be big trouble.

Shane and Morgan paid no attention to this movement. They paid attention only to one another. Sam Grafton noticed the silence in the saloon and came through from the store. He looked coldly round him and saw what was happening. Then he walked up to the bar.

Sam took a shotgun from under the bar and put it on top of the bar. His voice showed that he thought that the fight was unfair.

'There will be no guns used, gentlemen,' he said. 'And all the damages will be paid for.'

Morgan nodded quickly in agreement, but he did not take his eyes off Shane. Red Marlin and Curly and the two others stood behind him ready for a fight.

Morgan came closer to Shane and stood about an arm's length away from him. His head was thrown forward. His fists were held lightly at his sides.

'No one beats up one of my boys and escapes,' he said to Shane. 'Now we are going to drive you out of this valley. But before we do, we are going to give you the worst beating up you have ever had in your life.'

'So you have it all planned,' said Shane. But even as he was speaking, he was moving. In one movement he picked up his half filled glass of whiskey from the bar and threw the whiskey in Morgan's eyes.

Morgan was blinded. With the whiskey in his eyes he could not see. His hands stretched forward to reach Shane, but Shane caught Morgan's hands and held them tightly. Then Shane dropped backwards on to the floor and pulled Morgan with him. As he fell back on the floor, Shane kicked both of his legs up with all his strength. His feet landed in Morgan's stomach, and Morgan went flying straight over Shane's head. Then Shane let go of Morgan's hands and Morgan went flying away across the room in among the tables and chairs.

Morgan lay where he was. The other four ran in at Shane. As they came towards him, Shane jumped up behind the nearest table. He pushed the table over so that they had to move round it. He was waiting for the first one to come round the edge of the table.

It was one of the new men who reached Shane first. Shane lifted his knee up into this cowboy's stomach with all his strength. The man screamed and fell on the floor. Then he started to crawl away towards the door. That was another one out of the fight.

Morgan was standing up again and was coming to join the other three. Now it was four against one. Curly tried to get hold of Shane in his arms. But Shane brought up his arms and hit Curly on the chin.

Then the other new man did a strange thing. He jumped high in the air, brought his knees up against his stomach and then kicked out hard at Shane's head. Shane was able to move a little to one side but one of the man's feet hit him hard on the shoulder.

Shane staggered back but he was still alert enough to catch the man's foot. He twisted the man's leg strongly and threw himself on the twisted leg as the man fell to the floor.

The man cried with great pain and crawled away. He did not want to fight any more. Now it was three against one.

As Shane fell on top of the man, Curly caught him in both arms and held him tightly. Shane jumped up and kicked back at Curly's leg. Curly staggered back and nearly fell. But Red Marlin came in to help Curly. He caught Shane in both arms and held him tightly.

Then Morgan saw a good chance. He had moved up behind Shane. Shane was busy fighting Curly and Red Marlin and did not see him. Morgan picked up a bottle from the bar. He came up behind Shane and hit him over the head with the bottle. He hit Shane so hard that the bottle broke and the whiskey ran down Shane's face.

Shane went unconscious for a few seconds. He would have fallen to the floor if Curly and Red Marlin had not been holding him. Curly and Red held Shane tighter as Shane began to move again.

'Hold him tight,' said Morgan and he punched Shane in the face with all his strength. Shane was able to pull his head a little to one side. But Morgan's fist caught him on the side of the cheek. Morgan was wearing a ring on one of his fingers.

This ring cut Shane's cheek and blood started to pour down his face.

'Hold him tight,' said Morgan again. He drew back his fist to give Shane another punch in the face. But Morgan never made that second punch. There was a sudden interruption. Father had joined in the fight.

POINTS FOR UNDERSTANDING

1. Did Shane and Joe relax now that Fletcher's men kept away from their farm?
2. Why did Bob not run to tell his father what was happening in the saloon?
3. What was the sudden interruption as Morgan was preparing to hit Shane for the second time?

13. Three Against Two

I was so busy watching what was happening in the saloon that I heard nothing behind me. Then suddenly father was at my side.

He was big and terrible. He was looking across the overturned table and scattered chairs at Shane. He saw the blood running down Shane's cheek. And he was angry. I had never seen father so angry before. He was filled with such anger that his body was shaking.

I never thought that father could move so fast. He was on them before they even knew he was in the room. He hit Morgan so hard that the huge man went flying across the floor.

Then father reached out one big hand and held Curly by the shoulder. I could see his fingers bite into Curly's flesh. He took hold of Curly's belt with his other hand and pulled him from Shane.

Then father lifted Curly off the ground and up in the air above his head. He swung round and threw Curly away from him. Curly flew through the air across the saloon and landed on a table. He landed so hard that the table smashed under him. Curly was lying on top of the smashed table on the floor. He tried to get up but fell back and lay there unconscious. Another man was out of the fight.

As soon as father pulled Curly away from Shane, Shane turned on Red Marlin. He punched him so fiercely that Red fell back and hit his head against the bar. He staggered up to his feet but he did not turn to face Shane. Red went to the doorway and staggered out of the saloon. Another man was out of the fight. Now only Morgan was left.

Morgan was standing up again in a corner at the back of the saloon and he looked uncertain. Father saw Red Marlin staggering out of the saloon and turned back to Morgan. He started to move towards him.

'Wait, Joe,' said Shane quickly. 'That man is mine.' He was at father's side and he put his hand on father's arm. 'First get them out of here,' he went on. And he nodded round to show father that I was standing in the doorway and mother was standing beside me.

Mother must have followed father and had seen the fighting. She stood with her mouth open and she was looking carefully at Shane.

'You take Bob and wait at the wagon,' father said to her.

Mother shook her head but did not move her eyes from Shane. Shane was now moving across the saloon to face Morgan.

'No, Joe,' she said, 'Shane is one of the family now. I want to watch this to the end.'

The three of us stood there and watched. Shane was like a cat following a mouse. He was ready and alert. He had forgotten us and the beaten men on the floor. He was looking straight at Morgan.

Morgan was taller and much broader than Shane. He was

known in the valley as a powerful fighter. But he did not like the situation he was in. He knew it was unwise to wait for Shane to come to him.

Morgan ran at Shane trying to beat the smaller man with his great weight. Shane quickly moved to one side and as Morgan went past, Shane smashed his fist into the side of Morgan's face. Morgan rushed at Shane again. Again Shane moved to one side and punched Morgan's head.

Again and again Morgan rushed but always Shane moved away. And each time Shane punched Morgan's head.

Morgan stopped. He realized that he could not beat Shane in this way. Morgan suddenly jumped at Shane and tried to catch him in his arms. Shane brought up his right hand and as Morgan rushed into him, Shane's fist caught Morgan full on the mouth and nose. It was the same punch that Ed Howells had spoken of when he was telling us how Shane had beaten up Chris.

Morgan's face was red and he was bleeding from the mouth and nose. He shouted out something in his anger and picked up a chair. He ran at Shane with the chair above his head. Shane tried to move to one side but this time Morgan was waiting for Shane to do that. Morgan moved to one side also and brought the chair down heavily on Shane's head.

Shane fell on the floor and lay still. Morgan forgot that Shane was clever. He thought he had beaten Shane and jumped on top of him where he was lying on the floor. Shane was expecting this. He moved very quickly to one side and jumped to his feet. Morgan fell heavily to the floor and Shane got behind him. Shane used his right fist like a hammer and brought it down with full force on the back of Morgan's neck behind his ear.

Morgan lay unconscious on the floor. The fight was over. For some time there was complete silence in the saloon. Morgan lay on the floor and Shane stood quite still. Only Shane's eyes were moving. He seemed to be asking if anyone else wanted to fight him.

Then Shane began to relax. Suddenly I realized how beaten he was. He was covered in blood and sweat. I could see even at a distance the lump on his head where Morgan had hit him with the bottle. And that was bleeding too.

Shane put his hand up to his head. Then he looked at it. His hand was covered in blood. He himself seemed to realize how beaten he was. He swayed slightly and started to move towards us. As he did so, he staggered and almost fell.

Mr Weir, one of the townsmen, walked towards Shane as if to help him. Shane saw him coming but he did not move. His eyes showed that he did not want any help from Mr Weir.

But when Shane reached father, he almost fell again. Father put his arm round Shane's wrist and held him up. Father was the one man that Shane would take any help from. He was too proud to take help from anyone except a really close friend like father.

Father turned to help Shane out to the wagon. As he did so, he spoke to Sam Grafton.

'Let me know the cost of the damages, Sam,' he said. 'I'll pay for them. You can put them on my bill.'

Mr Grafton surprised me. 'I'm going to ask Fletcher to pay,' he said. 'And I'll see that he does pay. I'll put the damages on his bill.'

Mr Weir surprised me even more. 'Listen to me, Starret,' he said. 'It's about time this town was more proud of itself. I'm going to collect money from the townsmen and we'll pay for the damages.'

Things were changed now. The townsmen had seen how father and Shane could fight against Fletcher. Now they were on our side.

But father refused both offers.

'Thanks,' he said, 'but none of you will pay. I will pay.'

'No, I'm wrong,' he said as if he had changed his mind. 'We will pay for the damages. Shane and me will pay for them.'

And both men stood there proudly. Shane was leaning on

father's arm but he still looked proud. Then father moved away and helped Shane to the wagon.

Mother and I followed. We wanted to lay Shane down in the back of the wagon but he refused. He climbed up and sat proudly between father and mother on the front seat and I sat at the side.

Then we drove off home.

POINTS FOR UNDERSTANDING

1. Why did Marian refuse to leave when Joe asked her to go out of the saloon?
2. Why were the townsmen now on the side of the homesteaders?
3. Who was going to pay for the damages?

14. We Have to Wait

When we arrived back at the farm, mother got busy in the kitchen. She put a pot of water on the fire to heat and she tore up some old shirts into strips of cloth.

Mother looked after Shane first. He was much more badly beaten up than father. She washed the cut on his head carefully and kindly. She wiped away all the blood and made sure that there were no pieces of broken glass in the cut.

When mother had finished looking after Shane, she turned to father.

'Take off that shirt, Joe,' she said. 'It's all torn down the back. I will see if I can repair it later.'

Then she changed her mind.

'No, I won't even repair it,' she said. 'I'll keep it in memory of a very, very brave man. You were wonderful, Joe. You fought so bravely.'

'It was nothing,' replied father. 'I got so angry when I saw those men holding Shane so that Morgan could hit him.'

Later in bed that night, I wondered why mother had praised father, but had not said a word of praise to Shane.

I thought I understood why. Shane had done what we would have expected him to do. It was not necessary to praise him.

But I wondered if there might be another reason. Perhaps mother wanted to show father that she still loved him. It was Shane that mother had watched so closely in the fight. And it was Shane that mother had looked after first when we got home. Mother might be afraid that father would think that she now loved Shane. Perhaps she was showing father that she still loved him.

After that fight we were not troubled by Fletcher's men at all. We did not see them on our side of the river or even on their own side. Even Ernie Wright, whose farm was nearest to their range, saw nothing of them.

We heard that Fletcher had gone away again. But no one knew why. Perhaps he had gone away on business about his contract.

Despite this, father and Shane were more alert than ever. They stayed even closer together at work. They did not work out in the fields so much and in the evenings we no longer sat out on the porch although it was still warm.

After dark we sat in the house with the lamps partly covered. This meant that anyone looking in would not see us so clearly. Also, father hung his rifle on two nails beside the kitchen door.

I was surprised that we were so careful. And so about a week later at dinner I asked father for a reason.

'Is there something else wrong?' I asked. 'Surely the fight is finished now that you and Shane have beaten Fletcher's men?'

'You may think that it's finished,' replied Shane, 'but you're wrong, Bobby boy, it's only just beginning.'

'That's right,' went on father, 'Fletcher has gone too far to stop now. He has to make sure that he wins this fight. If he can make us leave our farm now, then the valley will be his for a long time. But if he cannot make us leave, then he is finished.'

'The townsmen are already beginning to support us,' father continued. 'Other homesteaders in distant places will hear the story of the fight. They will start thinking of moving here. If that happens, it will be the end of Fletcher's power in the valley.'

'Why doesn't Fletcher do something then?' I replied. 'It seems very quiet in the valley now.'

'It may seem like that to you,' interrupted Shane. And he spoke to me as if I was a grown up man. I really liked him when he spoke to me like that.

'You see, Bob,' he went on, 'Fletcher has shown everyone that he is determined to make us leave. Your father and I have beaten all his men and all the valley knows about it. He can't stop now. He must try something else. It's when things are quiet that you've got to be most careful.'

Mother looked unhappy.

'I suppose that you two are right,' she said, 'But does there have to be more fighting?'

'I don't think that there will be more fighting like the other night,' said father. 'Fletcher knows better now.'

'He knows it won't work,' said Shane. 'We have shown him that we can beat his men in a fist fight. Now he must try something else.'

'Yes, he'll have to try some other way,' said father. 'Perhaps he has gone to the government offices. He may try to prove that all the land in the valley belongs to him.'

'Yes . . .', said Shane doubtfully. 'He could be doing that. But there are other ways. It all depends on how mean Fletcher is. I think he is very mean and will do anything.'

62

'I suppose that you have met men like him in your life before,' said father.

Shane looked out of the window and did not reply to father's question.

'There's one thing that I'm sure of,' said Shane after a long pause. 'Once Fletcher has decided to do something, he will do it quickly. We won't have long to wait.'

'I wish that I was as patient as you,' said father. 'I don't like this waiting.'

POINTS FOR UNDERSTANDING

1. Why was Bob puzzled by the care taken by his father and Shane?
2. What did Bob's father say to him when Bob asked 'surely the whole business is finished?'?
3. What did Joe think that Fletcher might do next?
4. Did Shane completely agree with Joe?

15. Stark Wilson Arrives

We did not have long to wait. The next day, while we were having supper, Henry Shipstead brought us the news. Fletcher had come back and he had not come back alone. There was another man with him.

Henry Shipstead came to tell us the news and Lew Johnson, another homesteader, came with him.

Lew Johnson had seen Fletcher and this other man arrive in town together. Lew said that the other man was the meanest looking man that he'd ever seen in his life.

He was tall and his shoulders were broad. His eyes were hard and cold. Under his smart black coat he wore two large pistols.

Lew had heard Fletcher speaking to one of his cowboys who had come to meet them.

'This is Wilson,' said Fletcher to his cowboy, 'Stark Wilson.'

The cowboy said hello to the new arrival and then they quickly left.

When I heard Lew tell us this new man's name, I thought that it was a strange name for a man to have. Stark is a word

64

that means something that is bare or empty or harsh.

Lew Johnson was worried when he saw this stranger arrive with Fletcher. He wondered who this man could be. So he went off to see Will Atkey in Grafton's saloon. Will heard more stories and knew more people than anyone else in the valley because he worked behind the bar and heard everyone talking.

When Lew Johnson told Will that the new man's name was Stark Wilson, he would not believe it at first. Lew then told Will how he had heard Fletcher telling one of his cowboys the new man's name. Will Atkey looked very unhappy and told Lew what he knew about Stark Wilson.

Stark Wilson was really bad. He was a gunman:[20] and a killer. He could draw a gun[21] as quickly with his left hand as with his right hand.

Will had heard that he had killed three men in Kansas and perhaps many more in other places. It took us some time to understand what had happened. Then slowly I realized that Fletcher had brought this killer to the valley to work for him.

POINTS FOR UNDERSTANDING

1. Why did Bob think that 'Stark' was a strange name?
2. What had Will Atkey heard about Stark Wilson?
3. Why had Fletcher brought Stark Wilson into the valley?

16. Ernie Wright is Killed

Lew Johnson was talking about the stranger – about how mean he looked and about how he had killed so many people. Henry Shipstead was sitting in a chair looking afraid. Father was smoking his pipe and looking thoughtful.

Suddenly there was an interruption. Shane spoke and he spoke in such a way that we all sat up and listened.

'When did they arrive?' he asked.

'Last night,' replied Lew Johnson.

'And you waited until tonight to tell us!' said Shane. His voice sounded very angry. 'What a fool you are,' Shane went on, speaking to Johnson. 'You're a farmer all right, Johnson. You're a farmer and that's what you'll be all your life. You'll never be a fighter. You should have come and told us immediately.'

Shane turned round suddenly to father.

'Quick, Joe,' he said, 'tell me who is the most foolish of the homesteaders. Who is the man who will lose his temper most easily?'

As Shane said this, I remembered Ernie Wright when Fletcher's men were insulting him about pigs and soda pop. Ernie had said that he could not keep his temper much longer. He had wanted to start a fight then.

And so I was not surprised when father said: 'Ernie Wright. He's the one who would lose his temper most quickly.'

'Start moving, Johnson,' said Shane. 'Get out to Ernie Wright's farm as quickly as you can and bring him here.'

'We're too late,' said Henry Shipstead, 'We saw Ernie Wright and Frank Torrey going into town as we came out here.'

Shane jumped to his feet and rushed to the door.

'What's the reason for the hurry?' asked Henry Shipstead.

Just as he spoke, there was the noise of a horse galloping towards our farm at full speed.

'This will be the answer to your question,' Shane said bitterly, turning to Henry Shipstead and Lew Johnson.

And it was the answer to Henry Shipstead's question.

The man riding the horse was Frank Torrey, another homesteader and a friend of Ernie Wright's. Frank jumped off his horse and came towards the porch where we were all standing. We had all rushed out behind Shane when we heard the sound of the horse coming.

When Frank saw father, he tried to shout. But he was so afraid and upset that his voice came out as a whisper.

'Ernie has been shot,' he said. 'They've killed him.'

Frank fell down on his knees on the steps of the porch. Father gently helped him to his feet and led him into the kitchen. Frank sat down on a chair shivering and looking very pale.

'They've killed him,' he said again. 'They killed Ernie and he didn't have a chance.'

It took Frank Torrey some time before he was able to tell us the story. He was terribly frightened. And he was ashamed of being so afraid.

At last Frank told us what had happened. He and Ernie Wright had been in town on business. After they had finished their business, Frank and Ernie went into Grafton's saloon for a drink.

Because everything had been so quiet, they were not expecting any trouble from Fletcher's men. They noticed Fletcher and the new man, Stark Wilson, playing cards at one of the tables. But they paid no attention to them. They did not think that there would be any trouble.

But Fletcher and Wilson must have been waiting for a chance like this. Fletcher got up from his seat and came over to where Frank and Ernie were standing by the bar. Wilson put his cards down on the table and sat where he was.

Fletcher greeted Frank and Ernie politely. Then he turned

away from Frank and began to speak to Ernie. Fletcher told Ernie that he needed the land on which Ernie had his farm. Fletcher said that the land was needed for shelters for his cattle during winter. He had a lot of cattle and he needed more space for winter shelters.

'I'm willing to give you a fair price,' Fletcher told Ernie. 'I'll give you three hundred dollars for your farm.'

Ernie knew that his farm was worth more than three hundred dollars. He had spent much more than that on his farm already. He became angry with Fletcher. Fletcher had spoken to him many times before. He had often tried to persuade Ernie to sell his farm. Now Ernie answered Fletcher rather sharply.

'No,' he said. 'I'm not selling my farm. Not now or ever.'

Fletcher turned round slightly and nodded to Wilson. Wilson sat where he was but looked coldly at Ernie and spoke in a way that made Frank shiver.

'I would change my mind if I were you,' said Wilson.

'This isn't your business,' said Ernie quickly. 'You have nothing to do with this.'

'I see that you haven't heard the news,' replied Wilson softly. 'I am Fletchers new business agent. I am looking after all his business affairs from now on. Anyway I can see you're a fool. But what can you expect from a farmer who keeps pigs.'

The old insult was back again. Fletcher had certainly told Wilson about the pigs. Fletcher had planned this so that Ernie would lose his temper.

'I haven't any pigs on my farm,' Ernie shouted at Wilson. 'And I have never had any.'

'Are you telling me that I'm wrong?' Wilson asked quietly.

'I'm telling you that you're a liar,' Ernie shouted in reply.

There was complete silence in the saloon. Wilson opened his coat to show his gun clearly to Ernie and to everyone in the saloon. The other men in the saloon moved back against the walls.

'There is no man alive who has called me a liar,' Wilson said quietly to Ernie. 'Say you are sorry or you'll crawl out of this saloon on your stomach.'

Ernie was now in a mixed state of anger and fear. He knew what Wilson meant. He was faced with a gun fight. He had to draw his gun faster than Wilson and kill Wilson before Wilson killed him. The fear in him made him want to creep quietly out of the saloon. But his anger made him stand where he was and hold himself erect.

Ernie moved to get his gun. As soon as Ernie moved his hand, Wilson had his gun in his hand as if by magic. Wilson's first shot made Ernie stagger back. The second shot made Ernie spin round and he fell to the floor. Ernie was dead.

POINTS FOR UNDERSTANDING

1. Why did Fletcher say that he needed more space for winter shelters?
2. What did Wilson say to Ernie Wright to make him angry?
3. What words tell you that Wilson could draw his gun very, very quickly?

17. Joe and Shane

The news of Ernie Wright's death had spread quickly through the valley. As Frank Torrey was sitting in our house telling us the story, most of the homesteaders had come into our kitchen. They all wanted to know what had happened.

Some of the homesteaders wanted to go and get a marshal. But others pointed out that the marshal was too far away. It would take three or four days to get him here.

Also they realized that Fletcher had planned the business cleverly. Wilson could say that he had killed Ernie in self-defence.[22] The other men in the saloon had seen Ernie moving his hand towards his gun. In those days gunfights were accepted. If someone tried to draw his gun on a man, and if the other man drew his gun more quickly and shot the first man, then it was called self-defence and not murder.

But in our hearts we all knew the truth. Stark Wilson was the fastest at drawing a gun in the valley. No one had a chance against him. The homesteaders were farmers and not gunmen. Then I remembered Shane.

Shane was standing looking out of the window into the darkness. He looked cold and bitter. There was the same look about him that I had noticed on the first day he came to our farm.

Shane suddenly turned round and interrupted the homesteaders' talk.

'Yes,' he said. And he said it in a way that made them all stop talking and listen. There was complete silence in the room as he spoke. 'This is murder. I know it is. We all know that it is murder. Ernie had no chance. He was a farmer and not a gunman.'

Shane was silent for a few moments but no one said a word until he spoke again.

'I want all of you to go to your homes,' he said. 'And stay inside. This doesn't concern you. Fletcher chose to kill Ernie first in order to make clear what he wants to do. Now he'll make for the one man in the valley who keeps you here. He'll go for the one man he must get rid of. The one man that stands between you homesteaders and Fletcher and Wilson. And that man is Joe Starret.'

I thought that I heard someone whisper: 'Joe Starret and Shane . . .' Perhaps it was mother. She was standing looking at father and Shane half proud of both of them and half afraid.

Father looked away and pretended to be busy with his pipe.

The homesteaders looked pleased and yet ashamed at the same time. They were pleased at what Shane had said. They did not want to fight. But they did not like the way that Shane had spoken to them.

'You seem to know a lot about gunmen,' one of them said. He was trying to suggest that Shane was a gunman himself.

'Yes, I do,' replied Shane coldly and bitterly. And he spoke in a way that showed that he was a gunman but was not happy about it.

Then I remembered the beautiful gun that I had seen in Shane's saddle-roll. And I knew then that this was the secret of his past life. Shane had been a gunman. But I also knew that Shane had never been a mean killer like Stark Wilson.

The homesteaders knew that it was dangerous to ask any more questions. They started to leave for their homes.

They were ready to leave the fight to father and Shane. They were good and honest men. But they were farmers not fighters. They would stay in the valley as long as father stayed. If father was forced to move out of the valley, they would leave too.

They said goodnight to father but hardly looked at Shane who stood by the window looking out into the darkness.

I was sent off to bed. I heard Shane shut the front door and go off to the barn where he slept. I don't think father and mother slept very much that night. I did not sleep very much myself. I was too worried about what was going to happen.

I could hear father and mother talking in the kitchen. But they talked so quietly that I could not hear what they were saying. But I knew what was troubling them. Should we leave or should we stay? If we left, father would feel that he had lost his life's work. If we stayed, father might get killed by Stark Wilson.

POINTS FOR UNDERSTANDING

1. Why could Wilson say that he had killed Ernie Wright in self-defence?
2. Why did Shane say that Fletcher would soon try to kill Joe Starret?
3. Why was it difficult for Joe Starret to decide whether to go or to stay?

18. Fletcher Comes to Visit

The next morning the sun was shining brightly. Father and Shane looked happier. They both rode off into town together to go to Ernie Wright's funeral. They sat down to dinner as soon as they got back. And they were pleased at what had happened in town.

'Yes,' said father, as we were finishing dinner. 'Ernie was given a good funeral. Grafton made a nice speech. The townsmen collected money for the funeral and we weren't allowed to pay anything. Nearly all the townsmen were there. They can see the danger that they are facing now. If Fletcher can use a gunman on us homesteaders, he can use one on the townsmen too.'

It was clear from what father said that the townsmen were now on our side. But what could they do to help us? Only father and Shane could stop Fletcher now.

As we were talking about the funeral, we suddenly heard the sound of horses approaching our farm.

We all stopped talking and I started to run to the window. I wanted to see who was coming. Shane quickly stopped me and made me sit down.

'That will be Fletcher,' Shane said. 'He will have heard that the townsmen are angry at the murder of Ernie Wright. He knows that he must act quickly. You mustn't do anything foolish, Joe. He won't want to try anything here. Don't let him make you angry.'

Father nodded at Shane in agreement and went to the door. He took the rifle off the nails and opened the door with the rifle in his hands. Then he went out on to the porch. Shane stood behind father and mother and I watched from the doorway.

There were four men on horseback in front of our farm. Fletcher and Wilson were side by side and there were two other cowboys behind them.

Fletcher was a tall man dressed in fine clothes. He had a short black beard and bright eyes. He looked mean and cruel.

Stark Wilson looked strong. He was sitting relaxed in the saddle. But he still looked alert in the way that Shane did. He was ready for trouble even when he looked most relaxed. He looked very sure of his own power.

Fletcher was smiling and friendly. Or he tried to appear to be. Perhaps he thought that he was winning and that he could do what he wanted with us.

'I'm sorry to trouble you, Starret,' he said. 'And I'm sorry about the unfortunate death of Wright last night. I wish that it hadn't happened. I really do. If people would only be sensible, there would be no need for shooting. Wright should never have called Mr Wilson a liar. That was a mistake.'

'It was,' said father slowly. 'But then Ernie Wright always did believe in telling the truth.'

I saw Wilson stiffen and sit up straight. I knew how brave father was. By replying in the way he had done, father had joined Ernie in calling Wilson a liar.

'Anyway, say what you want to say, Fletcher,' continued father. 'And then get off my land as quickly as you can.'

Fletcher was still smiling. He was trying very hard to appear pleasant. 'There's no need for us to argue, Starret,' he said. 'You have worked on a big cattle range and you understand my position. I need all the land I can get now. I must have the land to get enough cattle for my contract with the Indians.'

'I've heard all that before,' replied father. 'You know what I think about it. If you have anything new to say, speak out quickly.'

'Well, I do have something new to say,' went on Fletcher. 'I want you to join me. I am getting rid of Morgan and I want to offer you his job as a foreman. And I'll give your man, Shane, a job too.'

Father was surprised. He had not expected anything like this. Father spoke softly to Shane who was standing behind him. But he did not take his eyes off Fletcher and Wilson for a moment. Then father spoke again.

'What about the other homesteaders?' he asked. 'What about Johnson and Shipstead and the others? Do they have to leave the valley?'

'They'll have to go,' replied Fletcher quietly, but with determination.

When Fletcher said this, father did not hesitate. 'No,' he said. 'If I stay, then they will have to stay too.'

A look of furious anger came over Fletcher's face and he started to turn to Wilson. I was sure that he was going to ask him to start shooting. Then he stopped himself. Fletcher was a clever man. He knew that he must make father lose his temper first. He must do the same to father as he had done to Ernie Wright.

He turned back to father again. 'I'll give you a thousand dollars for your farm, Starret,' he said.

'No,' replied father. 'I am not selling this land.'

'Then I'll make you a better offer,' continued Fletcher. 'I'll give you twelve hundred dollars. You don't need to decide now. I'll be waiting for you in Grafton's saloon tonight. And I hope that you will be more sensible than you are now.'

With these words he turned his horse round and rode off. Wilson and the other two cowboys followed behind him.

POINTS FOR UNDERSTANDING

1. Why were the townsmen afraid?
2. Why did Joe refuse Fletcher's offer of a job?
3. Where would Fletcher be waiting for Joe that evening?

19. Shane Puts on his Gun

We all stood on the porch in silence. Father stood at the front with his rifle raised. Shane stood behind him and mother was in the doorway. I moved up beside father.

I broke the silence by asking a question. 'Are you going to sell our farm?' I asked.

As soon as I spoke, I knew that I had asked a foolish question. There was only one answer that father could give. He had to say no. Then Wilson would have his chance.

No one answered my question. Father sat down on the top step of the porch and lit his pipe. As he smoked, he looked out over the river to the beautiful hills in the distance.

Shane sat on a chair on the porch and looked deep in thought. I went into the kitchen with mother and helped her clean up. When we finished, we went back to the porch. The two men were sitting in the same position as before.

I sat down beside father and he put his hand on my head. He turned to me and spoke sadly. He spoke to me as if I was no longer a boy but a man.

'This is going to be hard for you, Bob,' he said. 'There is no other way. I must go to Grafton's saloon and face Fletcher and Wilson. Wilson can draw his gun faster than me. I know that. But I have enough strength in my body to get him as well. Then the other homesteaders can stay here and you can stay here with your mother and Shane.'

As he said these words, there was a sharp sound behind us on the porch. Shane had stood up so suddenly that he had knocked over the chair that he had been sitting on.

His fists were held tightly and he was shaking. You could see that he had made a terrible decision. He was going to do something that he felt he had to do. But you could see that he did not want to do it.

Shane walked down the steps of the porch and walked over to the barn like a man in a dream.

Mother went over to father and they held one another tightly.

'He must not do it,' said mother. 'He doesn't want to do it.'

'I know that he must not do it,' replied father. 'You must look after him, Marian. You keep him here while I go to Grafton's.'

I did not understand at first what they were talking about. Then Shane came out of the barn and came towards us. And as soon as I saw Shane I understood what they had been talking about.

He was the same Shane, but he was also different. He looked more alert and more terrible than I had ever seen him before. He looked even more terrible than when he was fighting Morgan at Grafton's.

Shane had put on his gun.

He had changed from his work clothes into the clothes that he had been wearing on the day he first came to our farm. And he wore his gun as if it were part of him. As if it was another arm or leg.

This was not the Shane that we had known during the summer months. And yet it was the same Shane, but somehow more complete. It was as if the gun was part of him that had been missing.

Now that he was no longer wearing his rough working clothes, he looked slim again. He stood in front of us looking slim and dark and dangerous.

As father had said, he was the most dangerous man that we had ever seen. And also he was the safest man that we had ever had in the house. I realized that both of these sayings were right. This was the real Shane that we had not yet seen.

'What kind of parents are you?' he said to father and mother. 'You haven't got supper ready for young Bob yet. And for yourselves too. I don't want any supper. I'm off to town. I've got some business to do there.'

Father looked straight at him. For a moment a light of hope came into his eyes and then it faded away.

'It won't do, Shane,' he said. 'It's my business, not yours. It is me that Fletcher is looking for, not you. Your offer is the finest offer that any man could make to another man. But I can't accept it. I must go there alone and face Fletcher.'

'You're completely wrong,' replied Shane. 'This is my business, not yours. Guns are my business. You're a farmer not a gunman. I am a gunman. I've been one all my life. I wanted to escape from it when I came here, but now I know that I can never escape.'

'You stay here and take care of Bob,' Shane continued. 'See that he gets the chance in life that I never had.'

'No I can't,' said father. 'It's my business. If I don't face up to Fletcher, I will never have the pride to look any man in the valley in the face again. Or woman.'

As he said these words, father looked to mother for help in this argument. But mother looked away from him. She loved them both, but she did not want father to go to town. She knew that it would end in his death.

Shane noticed her looking away and he knew what she wanted. Shane had to go to face Fletcher. Mother wanted him to go.

Father sat down at the table and looked very determined.

'I am going and I am going alone,' he repeated.

'You're wrong, Joe,' repeated Shane. 'Even if you kill Wilson, you will not be able to kill Fletcher as well. Then Fletcher can easily bring another gunman into the valley and you will die without helping the homesteaders.'

'It doesn't matter what you say,' replied father. 'I am going into town.'

As Shane was speaking, he had moved round behind father who was still sitting at the table.

'No,' said Shane. 'There is no man alive who can tell me what to do. Not even you, Joe Starret.'

As he was speaking, he quietly brought out his gun. Before father could see what was happening, Shane brought down the handle of the gun sharply on the back of father's head behind his ear.

Father fell forward on the table. Shane had knocked him unconscious. Shane then put his gun away and gently moved father's head to one side so that he looked as if he was sleeping peacefully. Then he turned to mother.

'I had to do it,' he said.

'I know,' replied mother. And she spoke as if she was sure that Shane had done the right thing.

'I knew that he was determined to go into town himself,'

said Shane. 'He couldn't have done anything else and still be Joe Starret.'

A look of great pride came into mother's eyes. She looked at father lying with his head on the table and at Shane standing in front of her.

'I know that you are doing this for both of us,' she said to Shane. 'And I am happier about that than about anything else.'

And even young as I was, I knew what she meant. She was half in love with Shane and she was afraid that Shane loved her. But now she knew that Shane loved her and respected father too. Shane was not doing this just for mother. He was doing it for mother and for father and for me.

POINTS FOR UNDERSTANDING

1. In what ways did Shane now look different?
2. What did Shane say that he had been all his life?
3. What could Fletcher do if Joe Starret killed Stark Wilson?
4. Why did Shane hit Joe Starret on the head?

20. Shane Goes to Town

Shane and mother looked at one another for a few moments in silence. Then Shane went out of the room and he had gone.

Nothing could have made me stay at home that night. Mother stood for some moments looking at the empty doorway through which Shane had disappeared. Then she turned to look after father.

As soon as I saw that she was busy with father, I crept quietly out of the door and ran towards the road.

But before I reached the road, I heard a noise. It was Shane coming out of the barn. And he was carrying his saddle-roll with all his things in it. My heart filled with sadness because I knew what that meant. When Shane had finished his business at Grafton's, he was going to leave us for ever.

Shane had come to our valley wanting to escape from being a gunman. When he went into Grafton's and fought with Wilson, everyone would know that he was a gunman. It would never be forgotten in the valley.

I had really grown up now. I felt so sad that Shane was leaving us. But I knew why he had to go.

Shane saw me immediately and I was afraid that he would send me back. He stood still for a few moments. Then he jumped up into the saddle, and when he was firmly seated, he pulled me up after him.

As we came up to Grafton's saloon, we saw Red Marlin on watch outside. He looked surprised when he saw Shane instead of father. He hurried up the porch and into the store.

Shane stopped in front of the porch and helped me down off the horse. Then he got down himself. He did not tie his horse to the rail. He left it standing there. The horse seemed to understand what it had to do. It stood there waiting for Shane. Then Shane walked up the steps of the porch.

Two of Fletcher's men were standing at the door. Shane went straight up to them.

'Where's Fletcher?' he asked.

One of them pointed into the saloon.

'Turn round both of you,' said Shane. 'Walk into the saloon and don't turn round again until you reach the bar.'

Although Shane did not have his gun in his hand, he spoke so coldly that the two men obeyed him. They walked with their backs to Shane right into the saloon and up to the bar. Shane walked behind them. When he got into the saloon, Shane stopped and looked round.

I hurried after him as quickly as I could. I took up my position on top of the box at the entrance. From there I could hear and see everything that happened in the saloon.

Sam Grafton had been in the store when Shane walked through into the saloon. He came over and stood right beside me. But he was so eager to watch what was happening in the saloon that he did not notice me on my box.

The big room was crowded. Nearly all the townsmen were there, but not one of the homesteaders. There were many new men there that I had never seen before. The room was so crowded that the men at the bar were standing close together side by side.

Some of Fletcher's men were sitting round a large table. But one chair was empty and a smoking cigar was lying in the ashtray in front of it. Someone had just left that chair.

Everyone in the saloon was looking at the slim, dark figure of Shane. He was standing just inside the saloon entrance. The only persons behind Shane were Sam Grafton and myself.

This was Shane as I always knew he would be. He was so sure of himself that no one in the saloon moved or spoke. There was complete silence in the room.

Shane's eyes searched the room. He seemed to notice the empty chair and the cigar. Then he noticed a man sitting by himself at a small table. This man had his hat pulled down over his face. I suddenly realized that it was Stark Wilson. I saw that Shane had noticed him too.

Shane's eyes moved further round the room. He was looking for someone else. Shane looked further round the room. He stopped when he saw Chris. Shane's face relaxed just a little. He gave a half smile towards Chris.

For a moment Chris looked embarrassed. Then he smiled at Shane in a very friendly way. He was showing by his smile that he had made up his mind. Chris was now on Shane's side.

But Shane's eyes were already moving on. He noticed Red Marlin standing in a corner near the bar. Then Shane suddenly looked round at Will Atkey who was standing behind the bar looking very afraid.

'Where's Fletcher?' asked Shane.

'I don't know. I don't know,' replied Will. And the shaking of his voice showed how afraid he was.

Shane swiftly turned back to Red Marlin.

'Where's Fletcher?' he asked again.

There was complete silence in the room. I felt as if there was a rope being pulled tighter and tighter. Something had to break.

POINTS FOR UNDERSTANDING

1. How did Bob know that Shane intended to leave the valley for ever?
2. Why was Shane going to leave the valley?
3. Who do you think had been sitting in the empty chair with a smoking cigar in front of it?
4. How did Chris show that he was now on Shane's side?

21. Shane Against Wilson and Fletcher

It was Stark Wilson who ended the silence in the saloon.

Wilson stood up suddenly and faced Shane.

'Where's Starret?' asked Wilson.

As soon as Wilson spoke, Shane moved towards the side of the room. But Wilson was moving too. He got into a good position near the bar with his back to a wall.

Shane saw that he was not in such a good position. He did not have a wall behind him and there was nothing in front of him to protect him.

I saw that Shane had noticed this but it did not worry him. He took a quick look round the saloon and up to the balcony which was empty. Then he faced Wilson.

The other men in the bar pushed one another to get to the opposite side of the saloon. Shane and Wilson were alone.

Wilson spoke again. 'Where's Starret?' he asked. Wilson seemed to think that no man would be brave enough to face him. But Shane did not seem to hear Wilson's question.

'I have a few things to say to Fletcher,' Shane said. 'But they can wait. I want to talk to you first, Wilson.'

Shane's words surprised Wilson. Wilson seemed to realize that he was facing a man who might be good with a gun.

'I have no argument with you,' Wilson said. 'My argument is with Starret. And it's Starret that I want.'

'You may want Starret,' replied Shane, 'but Starret isn't here. I have come to tell you that your days as a gunman are finished!'

Wilson began to understand what was happening. This quiet man was treating Wilson just as Wilson had treated Ernie Wright. Shane was pushing Wilson to draw his gun first.

Wilson was not afraid but he was surprised. It was probably the first time in his life that any man had treated him in the way that Shane was treating him now.

'I'm waiting, Wilson,' said Shane. 'Don't you want to ask me if I am a pig farmer?'

There was complete silence in the saloon again. Again I felt that it was like a rope being pulled tighter and tighter. Something had to break.

Shane's insult succeeded. It was Wilson who moved first. But as soon as Wilson moved his hand, Shane's gun was in his hand and he fired. Wilson was fast too. Two two shots rang out almost at the same time.

But it was Shane's shot that hit Wilson first. Wilson's gun fell to the floor. Shane's shot had shattered Wilson's right arm. Wilson's shot had just hit the side of Shane's arm.

Wilson's eyes showed that he could not believe what had happened. He stood there with blood pouring from his arm.

Then he moved to get out his other gun with his left hand. But before Wilson's hand reached the gun, Shane fired again. This time the shot went straight to Wilson's heart. Wilson dropped to the floor. He was dead. His killing days were over.

'I gave him his chance,' said Shane sadly.

The silence in the saloon was broken. The men were beginning to speak to one another in wonder. They had never in their lives seen a man drawing a gun as fast as Shane.

Then there was a sudden loud interruption. A gun fired again. And the wind from the bullet seemed to make Shane's shirt move.

Shane seemed to know immediately where the shot had come from. In one movement he dropped to the floor and raised his hand towards the balcony. Shane's shot rang out with the raising of his hand. He hit Fletcher who was standing on the balcony with a rifle.

Fletcher never fired a shot again. He fell forward and broke the rail round the balcony. With a crash his dead body fell to the floor of the saloon.

POINTS FOR UNDERSTANDING

1. Was Wilson afraid of Shane?
2. When Shane came into the saloon he noticed the balcony. Why was this useful to him later?

22. Shane Goes Away

After the loud noise made by Fletcher's body hitting the floor of the saloon, there was complete silence. No one could believe that a man could move as fast as Shane had done.

It was Shane's voice that now broke the absolute silence in the room.

'Well,' he said. 'That finished it. There will be no more trouble in this valley.'

The blood was dripping down Shane's arm from the cut made by Wilson's shot. But Shane did not seem to notice it.

'I am going away now,' Shane said quietly and coldly to the crowd of men in the saloon. 'And I don't want anyone to follow me.'

All the men stood silent and afraid. Not one of them moved as Shane turned round and walked past me to the door.

I was so surprised that I could not move for a few moments. Then I rushed out on to the porch. Shane was already on his horse and moving away.

'Goodbye, Shane,' I shouted. And tears were filling my eyes.

Shane stopped his horse and looked round. 'Goodbye, Bob,' he said. 'Look after your mother and father.'

His voice was full of love and kindness. This was the other Shane that I knew so well – full of kindness and goodness.

He turned round again and rode off slowly into the darkness.

I stood there on the porch. The tears were now running down my cheeks. For five minutes no one in the saloon dared move. Then suddenly they were all talking and shouting and running out on to the porch.

It was Chris who found me standing on the porch crying.

'Come on, Bob,' said Chris. 'Remember that you would not like Shane to see you like that. Brave men don't cry.'

I wiped my eyes and stopped crying. I thought about

Shane. I had to be brave and be a man.

Chris got up on to his horse and lifted me up in front of him.

'I'm taking you home,' he said. 'And I'm going to live there with you and your mother and father. I will never be a man like Shane, but I will work with your father to make his farm the best farm in the valley.'

Then we rode off home together.

POINTS FOR UNDERSTANDING

1. On page 25, Joe warned Bob not to get too fond of Shane. Had Joe been right to give this warning?
2. What did Chris do at the end?

Glossary

1. *to breed cattle* – page vi
   to produce cattle and to feed them until they can be sold for meat.

2. *cowboy* – page 1
   a man who looks after cattle, cows and other animals on a ranch.

3. *head of cattle* – page 3
   a number of cattle together, here thirty cattle.

4. *to make up one's mind* – page 6
   to think about something and then to decide what you are going to do.

5. *saddle-roll* – page 6
   a roll of blankets, clothes and other things, strapped to the saddle of a horse. See the illustration on page 2.

6. *landlord* – page 8
   a man who owns land which he lets other people use for a payment of money.

7. *boarding house* – page 20
   a house like a small hotel where you pay money for a room and for food.

8. *to be beaten up* – page 21
   to be hit, kicked or punched very severely.

9. *to drive someone away* – page 21
   to make him leave.

10. *to take aim* – page 24
    to point a gun at someone in order to hit him with the bullet.

11. *to get fond of* – page 25
    to begin to like someone very much.

12. *contract* – page 26

>   an agreement to buy or sell something at a fixed price.

13. *a fair price* – page 27

>   an amount of money which something is worth. If a hat is worth one pound, then one pound is a fair price to pay for it.

14. *marshal* – page 27

>   an official like a policeman – he looks after a huge district.

15. *sheriff* – page 27

>   an official like a policeman – he looks after a town or village.

16. *to lose one's temper* – page 42

>   to be very angry and to do something because you are angry. If you are angry with someone and you hit him you are 'losing your temper'. If you are angry but you do not do anything, then you are 'keeping your temper'.

17. *to duck* – page 45

>   to bend down fast. If someone throws a bottle at you, you might duck so that the bottle does not hit you.

18. *to stagger* – page 45

>   to walk in a shaky manner moving from side to side.

19. *unconscious* – page 47

>   unable to hear, see or say anything because someone has hit you or because you are ill.

20. *gunman* – page 65

>   a person who is paid for shooting people.

21. *to draw a gun* – page 65

>   to pull out a gun and be ready to use it.

22. *self-defence* – page 70

>   to kill a person in self-defence is to kill him because he is trying to kill you.